# *Gettysburg*
## *The Field of Glory*

*By*

*CW Whitehair*

All rights reserved. No part of this book shall be reproduced or transmitted in any form or by any means electronic, mechanical, magnetic, photographic, including photocopying, recording or any information storage and retrieval system, without permission of the publisher and author. No patent liability is assumed with respect to the use of the information-contained herin. Although every precaution has been taken in this book, the publisher and author assume no responsibility for errors or omissions. Neither in any liability assumed for damages resulting from the use of the information contained herein.

Copyrighted 2010 by CW Whitehair
ISBN: 9781793923790

## *Acknowledgements*

As always, it was a pleasure and adventure writing ***Gettysburg: The Field of Glory***. No historian or author can put into words or describe the images or carnage that took place along Cemetery and Seminary Ridges on the afternoon of July 3, 1863. The best we can do is piece together all of the soldiers' eyewitness accounts and make the best effort in telling their story. In accomplishing this task this publication would not have been possible if it were not for the assistance of other individuals.

First, I would like to thank the staff at the Old Charles Town Library for their assistance, allowing me to spend hours searching through the ***Virginia Regimental Series*** collection in the Thornton Perry Room. I would like to also express a special token of my expression to Don Burgess. Don was instrumental in helping me locate the Papers of Randolph A. Shotwell at the Hathi Trust Library. Private Shotwell served with the 8th Virginia Infantry.

Joe Mieczkowski, who is a good friend and Licensed Battlefield Guide for the Gettysburg National Park read the chapters on Gettysburg. To him I am in debt and appreciate his assistance for reading the manuscript. Thank you, Joe.

I would also like to thank my mother, Virginia Whitehair for the use of the Russell family genealogy, and sharing my family's heritage over a cup of coffee on an early Thursday morning.

I would like to thank my good friend and fellow historian and author Bob O'Connor of ***The Virginian Who Might Have Saved Lincoln.*** Bob read the manuscript for historical accuracy and his input is greatly appreciated.

It is always important to have period photographs in a book. Some times they are the most difficult to find. I would like to thank the staffs at the Harpers Ferry Historical Association, Library of Congress, National Archives and a special thanks goes to Sue Boardman for the Gettysburg battlefield photographs.

An author always wants the best product that he can offer to the public. For this, I want to thank Arlene Pombo. Arlene's insight in editing the manuscript and meticulous eyes for detail has made this work enjoyable for the reader.

Finally, I would like to thank my wife Rhonda-Lee for reading the manuscript, sharing insight, and critiquing me on putting it together, but also her love, inspiration, and encouragement to see the project to completion.

## *Introduction*

I was born in a place called Between the Hills in Northwestern Loudoun County. Between the Hills or, as some of the locals called it, Loudoun Heights, is about three miles from Harpers Ferry, West Virginia. Many of the family members on my mother's side were also born at Between the Hills in an old rustic stone dwelling along what we used to call Russell's Ridge. I say Russell's Ridge because my ancestors, the Russell family, once owned all of the property in that particular area. When my Grandmother Daisy Russell married my Grandfather Harry Wiles she inherited all the Russell property.

I have always been interested in my family's heritage, especially when it came to America's Civil War. On my father's side of the family, most of my family members were loyal to the Union. Eleven of them fought for different infantry and cavalry regimental organizations under Major-General George Crook and the Army of West Virginia. When the Army of West Virginia was integrated into the Army of the Shenandoah under Major-General Philip Sheridan, they served honorably at such places as Third Winchester, Fisher's Hill, and Cedar Creek.

My mother's side of the family fought for the Southern Confederacy. There were two. James from Waterford, Virginia, who fought with Company A, Hillsborough Border Guards of the 8th Virginia Infantry from Loudoun County. My other relative, Jonathan Russell, was from Between the Hills. There is little known about his life.

I found out about Jonathan Russell through my grandmother, Daisy Russell Wiles. Back in 1965, she began receiving letters from a Mr. Bert Russell from California, who was looking for information pertaining to my grandmother's members of the family. He was a family member working on the Russell family genealogy. The letters continued for a few years and then one day he came to visit my grandmother.

The genealogy that appears in this text from Bert Russell is the original given to my grandmother. Bert's great grandfather and my grandmother's great grandfather were from the same bloodline. Jonathan, Bert's great grandfather, was said to have served as a Confederate soldier, although we have never been able to determine his regimental affiliation.

Israel Russell, who appears in this text is my great-great uncle through my Grandmother Wile's bloodline. Prior to the Civil War, Israel was a Justice of the Peace at Harpers Ferry. Israel was one of John Brown's hostages during Brown's infamous raid on Harpers Ferry in October of 1859. During the Civil War, he remained faithful to the Union.

Joseph Russell is also from my Grandmother Wile's direct bloodline. Like his brother Israel, he was loyal to the Union. He did not serve in the Union army as a soldier.

Occasionally, Joseph did serve the Union Cause by spying and passing useful intelligence on Southern activities to the various Union commanding officers at Harpers Ferry during the war.

In ***Gettysburg: The Field of Glory***, all of the events are true and accurate. I used Jonathan Russell to tell the story of the third day's fighting at Gettysburg instead of James Russell. Although James participated in Pickett's Charge, he did not make it all the way to the stonewall fence where some of the most bloody and savage fighting took place during the Battle of Gettysburg. He was captured at Gettysburg and imprisoned at Fort Delaware before being exchanged on October 31, 1864. I used Jonathan because I wanted to describe all of the events from the different regimental histories and diaries used in this text.

***Gettysburg: The Field of Glory*** was taken from various diaries, letters, regimental histories, The Official Records of the Union and Confederate Armies, The Southern Historical Society Papers, and period newspapers. The eyewitness accounts are very real and very descriptive. Period photographs of participants and locations have been included as well as all historical references, which are located in the back of the book for the reader's review.

## *Prologue*

For three years the Civil War had raged across the country, costing thousands of casualties, the destruction of property, and causing a profound effect upon every family living in the North and South.

Citizens in the North were becoming weary of the war and the continuous loss of lives in the Northern armies. Some were calling for peace with the Southern Confederacy.

One individual group was known as Copperheads. The Copperhead movement was made up mostly of Northern Democrats who called for a termination of the war, peace with the Southern Confederacy, and President Lincoln ousted from power. They were an important instrument to the Southern Confederacy and its independence because of their strong stance, powerful connections, and public opinion.

It was quite different in President Abraham Lincoln's administration. The Federal armies had suffered enormous casualties. There was a consensus to end the war among Copperheads and other influential citizens from the Northern states, but President Lincoln still wanted to continue the war until the insurgency was defeated and the nation reunited.

President Lincoln believed that the eleven rebellious states making up the Southern Confederacy were in revolt against the United States. Many Northern politicians did not believe the Federal Constitution gave an individual state the right to secede from the Union. Secession was an unlawful act and if necessary, conquering the Southern Confederacy would be the only answer.

The real war was on the front lines. In the western theater, the Southern forces led by Lieutenant-General John Pemberton were not winning as many victories as General Robert E. Lee and the Army of Northern Virginia in the east. In late June 1863, Pemberton's forces were trying desperately to maintain their hold on Vicksburg, Mississippi.

Vicksburg was the last major Confederate stronghold. As long as General Pemberton and his 28,000-man army could control the Mississippi River fortress, they could deprive Major-General Ulysses S. Grant and his Army of the Tennessee complete control of the river and from splitting the Southern Confederacy in two. General Grant had already won a series of victories in the campaign. He was victorious at Champion Hill, Raymond, and had also captured the capitol of Jackson. Vicksburg was the last major point of resistance along the Mississippi River. Governor John Pettus wrote President Jefferson Davis in Richmond: "Hour of trial is upon us. We look to you for assistance. Let it be speedy." General Pemberton believed Vicksburg to be the "most important point in the Confederacy."

Pressure was mounting on Jefferson Davis and his cabinet to relieve the besieged Confederate army under General Pemberton at Vicksburg. General Joseph Johnston was ordered to make the attempt to relieve General Pemberton, but claimed that the enemy had cut him and his forces off from offering relief to Pemberton's army.

Confederate Secretary of War James Seddon believed that reinforcing General Braxton Bragg's army, which was operating in Tennessee, was the answer to the Vicksburg dilemma. Secretary Seddon hoped General Bragg's forces, with reinforcements from General Lee's army, could strike north into Kentucky. General Grant would have no alternative but to turn and meet the threat, thus relieving the pressure on Vicksburg.

It was quite different for General Lee and the Army of Northern Virginia. Over the last year they had won major victories at Fredericksburg and Chancellorsville, inflicting heavy casualties on the Army of the Potomac. Since the beginning of the war, Lee's army had seen the ascension of three different Federal commanding officers in the east only to see them relieved of their command. Outnumbered, the Army of Northern Virginia continued to enjoy domination over the Army of the Potomac, but that was soon to change at *Gettysburg: The Field of Glory.*

Just two weeks after his victory at Chancellorsville, General Lee had several discussions with President Davis at his office in Richmond for another invasion of the North. General Lee's initiative was the same as Seddon's proposal but not sending troops from the Army of Northern Virginia. General Lee's intelligence after Chancellorsville suggested that the Federal army was reinforcing. General Lee believed it would be difficult to send General Bragg reinforcements from the Army of Northern Virginia, and argued "Virginia was the theater of action" and "his army, if possible, should be strengthened." If General Lee's forces were sent west, then it could possibly place Richmond and his army at risk.

Another consideration was that General Lee didn't want to fight another major engagement in Virginia. His army had suffered from hunger and he wanted to give the farmers time to plant crops. Virginia had been ravaged by three years of Civil War. General Lee believed that being aggressive and taking the war to the north would not only help fill empty stomachs, but would have a profound effect upon the critical situation and events unfolding at Vicksburg.

There was another consideration that convinced General Lee that the time for invasion of Northern soil was ripe. General Lee knew some of the experienced Federal regiments were mustering out of the service and the Federal army would have to rely on new and untested recruits to fill its ranks. They would not be a match for his experienced and battle-hardened veterans.

General Lee had also taken 6,000 prisoners at Chancellorsville and believed the Army of the Potomac was greatly demoralized. On June 9, 1863, Major-General George Meade, commanding the Fifth Corps of the Army of the Potomac, wrote his wife: "The army is weakened, and its morale not so good as at the last battle, and the enemy are undoubtedly stronger and in better morale."

On June 28, 1863, General Meade replaced Major-General Joseph Hooker as the commanding officer of the Army of the Potomac, leading it through the conflict at Gettysburg. General Meade was taking command of an army that was in the early stages of a campaign. He was an excellent corps commander, but would he be up to the challenges, emotional stress, and struggle of leading a 97,000-man army in a major battle? For General Lee there was no better time for invasion of Northern soil than now.

In June of 1863, Robert E. Lee was the most successful general in the Confederacy. General Lee was a brilliant tactician and enjoyed the respect and admiration of President Jefferson Davis and his Cabinet. President Davis and Secretary of War Seddon both agreed with General Lee's plan for a Northern invasion. Secretary Seddon wrote General Lee: "I concur entirely in your views of the importance of aggressive movements by your army."

Confidence was at its highest level during the war among the rank and file of General Lee's army when the decision was made to invade Northern soil for the second time in nine months. Major-General William Dorsey Pender of North Carolina, commanding a division in Lieutenant-General A. P. Hill's Third Corps, wrote his wife: "I feel that we are taking a very important step, but see no reason why we should not be successful. We have a large army that is in splendid condition and spirit." Lieutenant- Colonel James Fremantle, a British observer from Her Majesty's Coldstream Guard, spent three months in the United States with Confederate forces. While marching into Pennsylvania, Colonel Fremantle had the opportunity to speak with officers and the regular foot soldier. He wrote in his diary: "Everyone, of course, speaks with confidence."

When it came to the Confederate soldiers that would be on the front lines and doing the fighting on Northern soil, they were very confident of the army's ability. Private French Harding, Company F, 31st Virginia Infantry, wrote to Maggie Hutton: "I think the surest plan is to depend upon our own resources. I am confident they are sufficient to meet our wants and feel certain if southern skill and bravery is not equal to the task before them, it is no use for France to offer her feeble assistance." Captain William Berkeley of Company D, 8th Virginia Infantry, wrote to his wife: "Gen. Lee's campaign has been very successful and I hope that a few weeks may bring the war to a happy conclusion." The army's confidence and ability to win victories over their adversary, the Army of the Potomac, appeared to be unbeatable.

On July 3, 1863, after two days of bloody fighting with massive casualties between the blue and gray, General Pickett's men crossed "The Valley of the Shadow of Death." They were very confident that they could drive the Federal defenders of the Second

Corps of the Army of the Potomac, under Major-General Winfield Scott Hancock, from its defensive position along Cemetery Ridge.

The Confederate soldiers believed this last final push against the Army of the Potomac's center would crumple its defenses. If this happened and the Federal army retreated, this would bring General Lee's army to the doorsteps of Washington or Baltimore. The war would possibly end, gaining the Southerners their independence. It was men from the 8th Virginia like Captain Berkeley, Lieutenant Benjamin Hutchinson, Privates James Russell, R. B. Sampson, and Randolph Shotwell who held to this belief and trust in their commander, General Robert E. Lee. They would be greatly disappointed. They would have their hopes of the termination of the war and their invincible confidence shattered, being immortalized at **Gettysburg: *The Field of Glory*.**

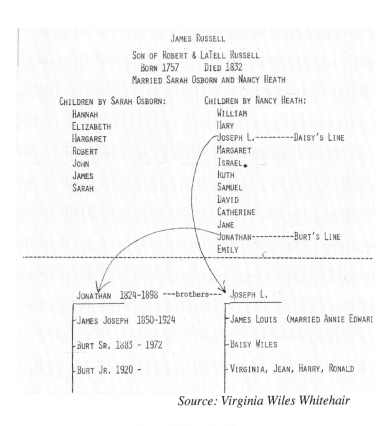

Source: Virginia Wiles Whitehair

**Russell Family Tree**

## Chapter One

My name is Jonathan Russell. I am a former Confederate soldier who served with the Army of Northern Virginia under the command of General Robert E. Lee. It has been fifteen years since the late War of Northern Aggression was concluded.

Quite a bit has transpired since that time. Slavery ceases to exist and is now outlawed according to the thirteenth amendment of the United States Constitution. I remember after the conflict when I first returned to Harpers Ferry, streams of water flowed down the center of the streets, and dreary hillsides showed only ragged growths of weeds. The town was half in ruins. The ruined bridge piers across the Shenandoah River were all that was left; still less remained of the old bridge across the Potomac River. All around the town were rubbish, filth, and stench. The former slaves were loitering about the streets of the town with no hopes of employment. Of course, it was that way for anyone living in the town, especially if it was discovered that you fought for the Confederacy. That all changed in time.

Everyone had learned Reconstruction was not just for the eleven rebellious Southern states, but for the Northern states as well. Before the war, the states enjoyed greater sovereignty. Now the United States Government was more central and had assumed greater power over the people. These were things that all of us had to get used too.

When I enlisted in the Confederate army in early May 1861 at Harpers Ferry, I believed soldiering would be an adventure and the war would be short in duration. Many, including myself, were greatly fooled by the resolve of the Northern people and President Abraham Lincoln. They possessed a fighting spirit and a determination to see the subjugation of the Southern people, no matter what means of war had to be used to accomplish their purpose. It was with determination the war became serious and bloody work for both sides. Oh, how the South did pay for its transgressions. The aftermath was just as trying on citizens as the conflict itself.

I had the unfortunate experience of fighting in many of the skirmishes and battles during the four years of what would be known as the bloodiest conflict this nation has endured. The horrible scenes I witnessed during the war are still engraved in my mind, and sometimes had an effect on the way I have lived my life. It was not only that way with me, but with others, both blue and gray, who experienced the same terrifying events and uncertainties that war supplied. The only experience that had eased my heart and mind since those frightful days, was my profession in Jesus Christ as my Savior. My Sarah's words and living testimony was what led me to the Hope.

It was not easy during the war witnessing the death and maiming of men who you had grown fond of and men who have, on more than one occasion, saved your life while fighting in close quarters. When soldiers share the same overwhelming struggles, sometimes impossible challenges, and enduring sacrifices, there is a strong and unbreakable bond that forms between them. It was much like being brothers.

How can I ever forget their screams of pain, the agonizing expressions of death, and the heroic way they sacrificed their lives for a Cause they believed to be righteous and just? On the field of glory, life can all come to a sudden and seemingly unmerciful end. It did for many of my close comrades at a place in Pennsylvania called Gettysburg. After many hard-fought battles, it was the fight that always stood out the most in my mind.

At Gettysburg, most of the Confederate soldiers who charged upon Cemetery Ridge that fateful day were full of spirit and confidence. We shared that confidence in General Lee. To us he was and will always be a great leader. There was not a soldier
within the ranks who did not believe the army as a whole was invincible. We overwhelmingly would have followed General Lee to the ends of the earth. Such as it was at Gettysburg.

The center of the Federal line was believed by General Lee to be the weakest point in the Federal defense, since the Federals had drawn reinforcements from their center to support their left and right flanks the previous day. If we could break through the center of the Federal line stretched along Cemetery Ridge, then hopefully it would collapse. One more powerful thrust and we would drive the Federals back toward Washington City. The war would end and we could all return home to our firesides. That was not to be.

It took some difficult times and struggles for me after the invasion of Northern soil to realize that the blood of Virginians would forever be mingled into the field of glory at Gettysburg, and that the war would not end in glorious victory for the Southern Confederacy. Instead, the bloodshed and uncertainties would continue, inflicting great pain and sorrow on families in both the North and South.

Now as I sit alone along Seminary Ridge, gazing out across the field where I witnessed the greatest amount of carnage that could possibly be known to man, it is trying for me to hold back my tears and emotions. This is the first time since that frightening day that I have returned to this place where the Demons of War were released on mankind. I hope no one now or ever experiences what us soldiers endured and struggled with here at Gettysburg.

Today is the anniversary of this great charge across this great field that I participated in as a soldier. It is quite a different place now than it was during the war. As I look across the once bloody battlefield, it is now a place of quiet and solitude. The trees are full of leaves, the farmers' fields are well manicured, and the air feels fresh. On Cemetery Hill, a large cemetery for the Union dead is now located. I will visit that place before my return to Between the Hills, Virginia.

The Round Tops, the Peach Orchard, and McPherson's Ridge, where heavy fighting took place on the first and second day, still remain. I am not trying to undermine the importance and furious struggles that took place at those locations between the two contending armies, but it was the fighting that took place between Cemetery and Seminary Ridges that defined this battle.

I came here at the prodding of my wife, Sarah, and my family to pen my recollections of events and experiences I endured leading up to that day. While sitting here there are still many memories and many images I can vividly see as they occurred.

How could I so easily forget?

It's painful and agonizing to relive this part of my life, especially seeing the Emmitsburg Road, the Codori farm, and the stone fence along Cemetery Ridge. So many times, I attempted to ignore it all, but found in the end that rejection of the fighting and killing was not the right way of doing things. My life has dramatically changed in many ways. Often, I think of those comrades who gave their lives on this field. Life is so valuable, but sometimes sacrificed so cheaply and needlessly on the battlefield. When events such as the fight at Gettysburg have an impact on one's life, it helps to change and shape the way that you look at matters and how you deal with future events. Events such as this engagement helped to accomplish that truth in my life. A large part of my life changed on Friday, July 3, 1863, at ***Gettysburg: The Field of Glory.***

## *Chapter Two*

I was born on May 9,1824, in northwestern Loudoun County, Virginia, at a place called Between the Hills by the locals. Between the Hills is a narrow valley that runs from Turneysville, near the Potomac River for about eight miles south to Hillsborough. It is only about a mile wide where our farm was located, bordered by the Blue Ridge Mountain on the west and the Short Hill Mountain to the east. As one travels south toward Hillsborough, the valley became wider with longer rolling ridges.

Between the Hills was filled with farms and homesteads surrounded by green rolling slopes, ridges, and plenty of streams filled with bass. On many evenings before the War of Northern Aggression, when I finished my work on the farm I enjoyed the solitude and peacefulness of fishing in its streams. After preaching on Sunday afternoons during the summer months, Sarah and I took our sons with us and enjoyed a picnic, or sometimes we would go alone and talk about family concerns or about our precious life together.

I was one of twelve children born to James and Nancy Heath Russell. I have six sisters named Mary, Margaret, Ruth, Jane, Catherine, and Emily. I have five brothers named William, Joseph, Israel, Samuel, David, and I am the youngest.

Most of my family members lived on a one hundred and thirty-five-acre farm that was handed down to my father by my grandfather, Robert. In 1806, my grandfather purchased the land from Ferdinando Fairfax at ten dollars an acre. Mr. Fairfax also sold the same amount of property to John Conard Jr. and John Demory. Our property stretched from the base of the Blue Ridge across Piney Run to the base of Short Hill Mountain.

In1845, my father gave me twenty acres to farm, since that was the vocation that most interested me. He also gave my brothers property, except Israel. Israel moved to Harpers Ferry to operate a store. For many years Israel was also the magistrate in Jefferson County. I would see him when occasionally I had to go to the Ferry on business or he came over for Sunday dinner.

Sarah and I had three sons, Owen, Harry, and Charles. They helped me farm and maintain the property. I proudly confess they were a blessing to me. Sarah was very active with the Ebenezer Methodist Episcopal Church along Short Hill Mountain. Often when some of the elderly or sick could not manage for themselves, she was one of the first to offer a helping hand or cook a meal to fill their hunger. It was through her Christian witness that she found reward in performing such good works. In the quiet of the evening near the fireside, Sarah knitted and spent time reading from the Holy Scriptures. If need be, Sarah could use a weapon just as good as any man.

Owen, Harry, and Charles were loyal to Sarah and me. Family had a very special place in their hearts. They were hard workers on the farm, performing any task that needed to be accomplished. Owen, the oldest, liked to read books about the human anatomy. His desires for a vocation were quite different from Harry's and Charles's. They wanted to be farmers. Owen wanted to be a physician.

On Russell's Ridge, which overlooked Piney Run, my brothers helped me build a five room, two-story dwelling for my family. The stone was taken from the western area of the property, located near my parent's home and where I was born. Our house was built North to South so that we could catch the summer breezes. The house had few windows on its western exterior. The reasoning was to avoid the windy winter days and nights.

Our property was very characteristic of what was found in most homesteads in northwestern Loudoun County. We built a small barn with a loft about fifty yards from the house to shelter our six horses, cows, and few hogs. We kept them enclosed in a small barnyard with a wooden fence. The few outbuildings constructed were frame and the springhouse were made of stone from the property. We also had a large chicken coop near the barn. The chickens supplied some of the biggest eggs that I had seen in these parts.

Our property included a large strawberry patch and peach and apple orchards. The ground was good and fertile, causing the fruit to be sweet and juicy. Some of the fruit and grapes that grew along the fence between the yard and garden made good wine. Quite often, Sarah spent long days preserving the fruit for the cold and wintry months. She would sing songs to pass the time. I knew in my heart she missed having a daughter, who she could teach the art of home making, and someone to talk to during her tasks.

The boys helped with the chores. They spent hours laboring in the large garden. Owen was always amazed by nature. When planting corn, he eagerly watched after planting the seeds. The seeds would sprout through the soil. First the stalk appeared, then the ears, then the full kernel in the ears. On the other hand, there were chores that did not please him or his brothers. You would think it would be cleaning the manure from the stalls and barnyard, but that was not true. It was pulling weeds in the garden near the house. It was the only job they complained about because it required them being on their hands and knees for long periods of time.

Sarah would not allow anyone to work in the area of the garden where the tomatoes, lettuce, and cucumbers were located. On many hot and oppressive mornings, she diligently labored for long uninterrupted hours. I can still see her on her hands and knees, wearing her straw hat, laboring and not speaking one complaining word.

The two-acre garden, chicken coop, and outbuildings were fenced with timber to keep our two dogs and animals such as deer and wildcat from destroying our crops. There were two ways to try and keep them from the garden. The first was a fence, which unfortunately always needed mending. It was Harry's job to keep up with it. Secondly, Harry liked to make the scarecrows to scare off the vultures and prey from invading our garden. The vultures were more- bold. Occasionally, they would swoop down on the scarecrows and try to get at the spicy leafs.

Workdays on the farm began with sunrise and most of the time continued until near dusk. This took place six and one-half days a week. Everyone knew their responsibilities because it depended on how much sustenance we would have for the winter months and how much money we had to spend from selling off some of our harvest.

On the farm we planted wheat, barley, and sometimes oats. It was hard labor during the summer months when the sun was beating down on us all day long, but the job had to be done. We rotated the different crops from field to field, never using the same field for more than one year for any certain crop. Some years corn was planted. Instead of traveling to Harpers Ferry where farmers from Loudoun County were given a discount for bringing their goods there to be ground, I continued the family tradition of giving my business to Joseph Conard. Joseph operated a grist mill about six-tenths of a mile from the Potomac River along a bend on Piney Run. His mill continued until the War of Northern Aggression began. I always remembered my friends and their loyalties and rewarded them with my business.

During the late autumn and winter months, we cut wood from the mountains. It took at least twenty cords to supply us with enough heat and cooking fuel. When the first autumn freeze arrived, the family butchered a hog to supply us with pork through the cold months. Apple butter was another provision we would make during that time of year. Throughout the day, family members would take turns stirring the apple butter in a large kettle, while someone else kept the fire hot. It was a time for family to work together and share their closeness. Sarah always knew how much cinnamon to add to make the apple butter tasty.

Since Owen was the oldest son, I often took him hunting with me. Most of the time, we hunted along the Blue Ridge Mountain. Early in the morning, we crossed Piney Run and climbed the mountain looking for squirrel, deer, bear, or any other meat that would supply the family's needs. It also gave us a chance to talk about his life and how he viewed the social issues that were inflaming our passions and times.

Owen was old enough to have a lady friend whose name was Mary Harris. She lived on a large farm about two miles south of our farm. Owen knew her from church and had become quite fond of her. Owen was a responsible young man. Quite often, Owen invited Mary to one of the barbecues that a neighbor would be hosting. The two were good dancers. They loved to dance to the Virginia Reel more than any other song.

Such was my family's life on a farm in Loudoun County. Unfortunately, our peaceful surroundings and serene life were about to be intruded upon and changed forever.

## *Chapter Three*

The closest town to our farm was Harpers Ferry. Harpers Ferry was about three miles, located at the convergence of the Shenandoah and Potomac Rivers. Back of its hills was the famous Shenandoah Valley where many Civil War battles were fought, lives lost, farms destroyed, and life changed forever.

Before the War of Northern Aggression, Harpers Ferry was a town of about three thousand four hundred citizens who equally hailed from the Northern as well as the Southern states. It wasn't like any other Southern community. Most of the town was made up of individuals who were white, although one hundred and fifty free people of color lived within the town limits.

The largest industry at Harpers Ferry was the manufacturing of weapons at the United States Armory on the Potomac River side of town and the Hall's Rifle Works located on the Shenandoah River side of town. Between the two armories, they manufactured over fifteen thousand weapons per year.

Other different types of industries were located at Harpers Ferry, such as a cotton and flourmill, but the weapons industry was the largest employer. Over half of the town's male population worked at one of the two armories.

Harpers Ferry had a thriving downtown merchants' district. Over forty merchants competed for the machinists', gunsmiths', and laborers' business. Most of those businesses were very profitable. The town's citizens were very traditional in their way of life. At the armory, the employees worked long and hard hours. They worked six days a week, making from one dollar to two dollars and eighty cents for a ten-hour workday. Sunday was a day of worship and rest.

The most memorable event for me surrounding Harpers Ferry was the flood of 1852. The winter of '51 and '52 had been exceedingly severe and the snow lay deep on the ground. I recall those cold and windy days when the boys and I had to split some extra wood. We thought winter would never end. That April, there were some very warm days with heavy rain falling. This caused the snow to melt rapidly and an unprecedented flood occurred as a result.

According to my brother Israel, who was living at Harpers Ferry during this time, flooding waters rushing down from the upper Valley of Virginia submerged the town. The citizens used large boats propelled with oars and poles along the principal streets. Sometimes it was difficult to navigate one's way because of all the debris floating on the water from the flooding. There was much damage to homes and businesses. It took time for the town to recover and much clean up was needed. Fortunately, there was no loss of life.

I can still recall when my older brother David and I were on the way to Harpers Ferry to visit Israel. During the journey, the water had been rushing down the mountain in streams, causing the Harpers Ferry Road to be quite muddy and slick. It was a slow journey. We didn't want to take a chance that one of the two horses pulling the wagon would fall and get injured.

As we came to the base of Loudoun Heights, which is part of the Blue Ridge overlooking Harpers Ferry from the Shenandoah River side, the level of water that had flooded the riverbank surprised us. I glanced over a cliff overlooking the Shenandoah, and found the river was up considerably. It was about a thirty-foot drop from the road to the river. The water was up well over half of the steep ledge. It was some time before the river returned to normal levels within its own riverbed. It left an impression on me as to how troublesome nature can be.

The next major event which took place in Harpers Ferry that would affect the whole area and produce severe consequences for our nation occurred on Sunday evening October 16, 1859. John Brown of Kansas fame, claiming to be the leader of a Provisional Army, arrived with twenty-one raiders. Captain Brown, as his raiders called him, had a reputation for fearless fighting in the dispute, which had taken place in Kansas. At the time, Kansas had to decide whether they would be admitted into the Union as a free state or a slave state. After great dispute and bloodshed, Kansas became a free state in January 1861.

When the alarm was sounded that Brown and his raiders had seized the armory and arsenal, a number of militia companies from the surrounding communities arrived to assist the angry citizens. The militia enclosed the armory grounds and had Brown in a perfect steel trap, killing and wounding many of his raiders, including his two sons.

During the raid, John Brown took hostages from among the town's citizens and some prominent individuals living near the town. One of those well-known citizens was Colonel Lewis Washington, the grand nephew of President George Washington. Another was John Alstadt, a German, who was also a slaveholder and owned a farm several miles west of town.

John Brown took hostages who were not as well known throughout Jefferson County as Colonel Washington, like my older brother, Israel. Brown's men had captured many citizens living in the town. John Brown held Israel and the other hostages in a fire engine house, which was located just inside of the armory ground entrance.

As the morning hours passed, there were too many hostages in the fire engine house. At one point according to my brother, there were sixty men confined in the little dwelling. All but nine were moved to an adjoining building, which was used as armory offices. Israel was not one of the fortunate citizens. Israel, along with eight others including Colonel Washington and Mr. Alstadt, remained in the engine house along with Brown and some of his raiders. I don't know the importance of keeping my brother as a hostage other than as I have already said, he was a Justice of the Peace.

There was still great excitement among the citizens. According to Israel, fighting had erupted off and on throughout the day. Some of the citizens, such as the town's mayor Mr. Fontaine Beckham, and several others had been killed. Most of Brown's raiders had been captured and killed during the exchanges, but still there was no termination to the stand-off.

John Brown asked for a volunteer to go out among the town's citizens and induce them to cease firing on the engine house because they were imperiling the lives of their friends, the prisoners. Brown promised that if the militiamen and citizens would not fire on him and his men, they would not fire on them. Israel undertook the dangerous task. I say dangerous because once one of the wooden doors of the engine house was opened, Israel knew he would possibly be fire upon because of the excited state of the armed citizens and militiamen. The citizens might think he was one of the raiders. He always was one to take a gamble.

Fortunately, Israel was not harmed and did intercede on behalf of John Brown with the citizen and militia leadership. The local officials did not care to accept Brown's request, but instead, kept up a steady skirmish with his raiders. Israel did not return to the engine house to deliver the news to Brown, but kept a constant vigil and observation of events that he told me about later.

According to Israel, by the next morning Colonel Robert E. Lee, then of the Regular United States Army, arrived from Washington City with ninety Marines for the purpose of capturing John Brown and to secure the freedom of the remaining hostages. When Brown refused to surrender, Colonel Lee gave one Virginia and one Maryland militia company the honor of storming the engine house. But they refused.

Colonel Lee gave the order and the Marines under the command of Lieutenant Israel Green rushed the engine house with a ladder. Once a small opening in a wooden door was made with the ladder, the Marines entered the building. They killed or captured the few raiders who remained. As for John Brown, he was wounded and captured.

The tally was high. Eighteen individuals on both sides had died for their convictions at the Harpers Ferry raid. Three of the four town citizens killed in the raid were good friends of Israel's. Thomas Boerly, an Irishman that owned a grocery store; George Turner, a graduate of the United States Military Academy at West Point, New York; and as I have already written, the town's well-respected mayor, Fountain Beckham. It's ironic that the first citizen killed in the raid was a former slave. Heyward Shepherd was just minding his own business, doing his job as a porter at the Baltimore and Ohio Railroad depot, when he was unmercifully shot down by one of Brown's men. This episode of the Brown raid always puzzled me.

John Brown was found guilty of his crimes and sentenced to

hang at the county seat of Charlestown on December 2, 1859. According to the *Virginia Free Press*, it was around 11:15 in the morning when Brown was hung. Before John Brown was taken to the gallows, he spoke to my brother, Israel. Brown said, "I know that the very errors by which my scheme was marred were decreed before the world was made. I had no more to do with the course I pursued than a shot leaving a cannon has to do with the spot where it shall fall."

Israel described John Brown as being tall, gaunt, gray and grim, with a countenance, though certainly not ferocious, yet terribly stern and menacing. John Brown and his raiders left an imposing influence not only on the citizens at Harpers Ferry and the surrounding area, but also the nation as a whole. Israel's friend, Joseph Berry, kept a chronicle of events at Harpers Ferry during the Brown raid and the Civil War. I am sure many of the citizens agreed with Joseph's views when he wrote, "Harpers Ferry enjoys the distinction of having been the scene of the first act in our fearful drama of civil war."

How true Joseph Berry's prophecy played out over the next eighteen months. The events surrounding John Brown's raid at Harpers Ferry would not only be the event that helped fuel the flames of civil war, but helped to fuel the bloody struggle that would take place at a little town four years later, called Gettysburg.

## *Chapter Four*

After John Brown was captured and executed by hanging in Charlestown, Harpers Ferry and the surrounding area remained in an excited state. Everyone knew the clouds of war were on the horizon, but we were not sure when all out hostilities would commence. I can still recall carrying a loaded pistol with me everywhere I went, even while working in the fields during the harvest. I allowed Owen to carry one while working with me on the farm, but not elsewhere. Harry and Charles wanted to carry a weapon, but Sarah and I believed the boys were too young at the ages of thirteen and twelve respectively.

Some nights after Brown's raid, I could not sleep because I did not know what harm might befall my family from runaway slaves or abolitionists. The times were unstable and many lived in fear. Often, late into the night, I sat near the fireside reading the Bible and occasionally looking out the windows. I was not the only person living in the valley who felt the same way. Mr. Levi Waters, who owned the next homestead, shared the same concerns for his family's safety. John Brown's raid was not only a trying time for the citizens living in Harpers Ferry, but also for families living in the surrounding area.

I recall reading in the *Virginia Free Press* militia companies or citizen soldiers began to form in most every community in the North as well as the South. Harpers Ferry was not any different than any other community when it came to forming a militia company. Recruiting took place at a fast rate in town and leaders were aggressive and inspirational for their reasoning. The citizen soldiers were not only armory employees, but also merchants, coopers, laborers, and blacksmiths.

Occasionally, Sarah and I invited Israel for Sunday dinner after we attended Sunday preaching. On his arrival one Sunday afternoon a few weeks after the raid, Israel told me about a gentleman residing in Pleasant Valley, near Harpers Ferry. This gentleman, whom he did not name, began circulating rumors that abolitionists and slaves had butchered citizens in a little community called Rohersville. Rohersville, Maryland, was located in Pleasant Valley about five miles from Harpers Ferry. The same gentleman circulated the same rumor at Sandy Hook, located at the southern end of the same valley along the Potomac River, about two miles from Harpers Ferry. Men, women, and children of Sandy Hook frantically rushed to Harpers Ferry seeking help because troops were still there. The rumor caused quite a wild stir among the town's citizens. The rumors proved to be false, but the excitement and state of anxiety continued for some time.

With all the unease, rumors, and great excitement, Israel said two militia companies were raised from employees at the Harpers Ferry Armory. Occasionally he watched them drill with all manner of weaponry, march and do their best to impress the town's citizens that they were capable of protecting them. They took turns guarding the Baltimore and Ohio Railroad bridge and the main roads leading into the town. During these times, Israel conversed on the streets with some of the town's citizens. Since he was the Justice of the Peace, they commented to him on how much better they slept at night knowing these men were armed and keeping a watchful eye and providing for their security.

Eventually the town leaders raised several more militia companies. Israel joined one of these organizations, the Floyd Guard. Armed with muskets and accouterments, fully clothed in uniforms, the citizen soldiers paraded down Shenandoah Street the first Saturday of each month. Israel said the young ladies waved their white handkerchiefs in the air, shouted patriotic slogans, and smiled at the soldiers. He liked that part of soldiering.

Once the militiamen arrived at the arsenal grounds, the soldiers would go through a number of military drills to the delight of the onlookers. Israel claimed that handling a weapon was awkward for him since it had been years since he used one. He didn't feel too badly because many of the new recruits were also having a difficult time executing the military drill with a weapon and keeping step in formation.

Afterward, the men enjoyed a barbecue of fried chicken and potato salad with their sweethearts, wives, and family. Once everyone's hunger had been satisfied, Israel and the men participated in competitive games with their women folk cheering them onto victory.

Israel said belonging to a local militia company was considered a civic duty to the community in which a male citizen resided. Every individual had a loyalty to his community. If for some reason one did not enlist in a militia company, that person was scrutinized for their lack of interest. If the reasoning was not good enough, then that person could be banished from any type of social gathering. By the beginning of the year in 1860, every able-bodied man living in Harpers Ferry belonged to one of the four militia companies.

One Friday afternoon in February, while visiting Harpers Ferry on business, Sarah and I stopped by Mr. Thomas Eagan's dry goods store along Shenandoah Street. Sarah wanted to purchase some writing paper, ink, and material to make the boys a few shirts. While Sarah was speaking to Mr. Eagan about the different patterns, color, and quality of the material, I was examining a pair of boots.

When the front door of the dry goods store opened, the hanging bell over the entranceway jingled. I turned and noticed Israel's close friend, Joseph Berry. I returned the boots to their proper place along the counter and walked over and exchanged salutations with Joseph, whom I had previously been introduced to by my brother. Joseph was a member of one of the Harpers Ferry militia organizations. As we spoke, I asked him about his experiences as a citizen soldier. According to Joseph, soldiering was not all fun. He liked the parades and the socials that followed, but standing along the muddy streets of the town on a windy winter night looking for prowling abolitionists was not a fun experience.

When the War of Northern Aggression occurred about eighteen months later, I knew Joseph Berry would not fight for either the blue or gray. Although he faithfully carried out his civic duty to the town by belonging to a militia company that eventually fought for the Southern Cause, he was a Unionist at heart. He continued to live in the town for the duration of the war. Joseph recorded events that took place in the community. Those events were military and actions that affected the lives of every citizen who chose to remain.

Throughout most of Jefferson County, many of the citizens expressed their loyalties to the South. It was not that way in Harpers Ferry. Half of the town's citizens had migrated from the Northern states. They worked at the armory. Not only had John Brown come from the North and lived nearby on the Kennedy farm in Maryland for a number of months, but also one of his raiders, John Cook, had lived among the town's citizens for eighteen months. Cook had spied on them, using the ruse as a schoolteacher and even married a respectable young lady, Mary Virginia Kennedy, to cover up his charade. Miss Kennedy knew nothing of his plans and association with John Brown.

After the raid, slave owners and individuals loyal to the South were concerned that more abolitionists were living in the area, waiting for the opportunity to create another attempted slave insurrection like Brown and his raiders. The Yankee way of life had never been popular at Harpers Ferry. Through their excitement and passions, town folks loyal to the South began to watch their neighbors from the North with more than a usual interest.

For all of us, it was a time of great consternation, many uncertainties, great distrust, and heated debate. I could visit Harpers Ferry at anytime during 1860 and men would stand on the street or in the saloons and argue the rights and wrongs of slavery and state sovereignty. Harpers Ferry, like most other communities along the Potomac River, was beginning to choose sides as our nation moved closer to an all out Civil War.

## *Chapter Five*

The Northwestern region of Loudoun County, Virginia was loyal to the Union. Between the Hills was a part of that district. In December 1860, South Carolina seceded from the Union. They were followed by six other lower Southern states through the course of the winter of 1861. Residents living in my area were quite angry over the actions that these lower Southern states undertook.

I was grieved over the question of secession from the Union because the consequences would have an effect not only on my life, but also of my family's. It appeared war would come, but no one was sure. Tensions were high, and compromise had all but died when Abraham Lincoln from Illinois was elected the sixteenth President of the United States. A Republican Congress, anxious to pass laws against the expansion of slavery, supported President Lincoln. This only inflamed the passions among the Southern people.

It was my hope that Virginia would not have to make a choice for who she would serve. Even though slavery existed within her boundaries, it was practiced with greater results in the lower Southern states where the cotton industry thrived. I was only a farmer. I did not own slaves and did not even agree with the practice of the institution. But I did not believe the United States Government had the right or the authority to order around and take away the liberties of Virginians or any other state for that matter.

Late in the day of April 12, 1861, the boys and I were repairing the roof on the barn when we received the news from Mr. Waters that South Carolina forces were bombarding Fort Sumter. At first, I was surprised and then my astonishment turned to grief. How many lives would be lost if there was not some resolution to end this crisis? If it continued, Virginia would have to make a choice. She could not remain neutral in this conflict. The answer came several days later after Fort Sumter surrendered.

On April 15, President Lincoln called for seventy-five thousand men to put down the rebellion. All the states were given a quota. Virginia was to supply a little over two thousand three hundred men. I recall over the winter months, delegates from all the counties in Virginia were sent to Richmond to decide if the state should withdraw from the Union. Twice they voted to keep her in the Union, but on April 17, under the leadership of former Governor Henry Wise, the delegation voted eighty-eight to fifty-five to secede from the Union.

The day after Virginia seceded from the Union, I recall the excitement created by the state militia marching on the town, which had been lightly defended by a small company of United States Regulars. When the Regulars realized they were outnumbered and it would be difficult to defend the government property, they attempted to torch the armory buildings. They failed in their efforts.

The Regulars did succeed in completely destroying the two arsenal buildings. Israel told me he witnessed men, women, and even children standing in two lines passing bayonets, accouterments, and rifles from the burning buildings, while other citizens and later Virginia militia tried to put out the flames. Israel said thousands of weapons were stored in the arsenal buildings and all were lost. I recall hearing the powder explosion at my farm around 10:00 o'clock that evening.

Passage of the Ordinance of Secession would not be final until the citizens of Virginia had the opportunity to vote on it. That happened on May 23. By a vote of thirty-nine to twenty-six, the residents of Between the Hills decided against Virginia seceding from the Union. When some of us men appeared to cast our votes, I gave great thought as I looked at each one of them. All of us were friends and neighbors. We attended the same barbecues, helped each other in hard times, and worshiped at the same church. What would be the possibility of fighting against each other? And if we did, how many would return home? After the war, it did cause a breach in life-long friendships that were never repaired.

When the secession vote was made final and Virginia was now in alliance with the new Southern Confederacy, I had to make a choice. Would I fight for the Union, the Southern Confederacy, or try and sit out the war? Over the next few days, Sarah and I spent long evening hours talking about the choices that confronted us. Even though her arguments were persuasive against me serving, I believed I had an obligation. For me honor as well as rights and family were at stake. I believed the Federal government was trying to restrict the rights of its people. The Republicans had come to office with new radical ideas that were not acceptable to me. Those ideas would have a future influence on my life and that of my family's.

I was greatly torn with the idea of taking up arms against the old flag. I just couldn't accept the current government in its present form. I decided to cast my lot with my state of Virginia where I was born and where my first loyalties were committed.

I had thought of going to Hillsborough and enlisting with the company of soldiers raised during the John Brown raid. Since Harpers Ferry was closer, and I enjoyed a number of acquaintances where I carried out my business, I decided that this is where I would go and enlist my services.

When it came time for me to depart on the morning of May 27, I found Sarah sitting quietly by the fireside, with a heart doubtless heavier than I knew. She was finishing a heavy shirt, which I was sure was for my use. When I said my farewell to her, Owen, Harry, and Charles entered the parlor. I encouraged them to help their mother run the farm, to obey her commands, and to respect her decisions. This they faithfully promised to do. Owen was the one that I depended on the most to be the example for the other two. My only concern was would they suffer retribution once it was known that I was serving with the state forces?

****

When I arrived at Harpers Ferry later that morning to enlist in the Confederate army, the town had already quickly changed in appearance. The armory was vacant of its workers. I noticed the twenty-two-building armory compound had suffered little damage from the fire of April 18. This was because town citizens and armory workers loyal to the Southern Cause came behind the Regulars and put out the powder train used to ignite the fire. The only buildings destroyed in the armory compound were the Carpenter Shop, Saw Mill, and Grinding Mill.

As I walked along Shenandoah Street, I noticed the citizens' ability to perform any type of business at the stores, shops, and bank had been totally disrupted and, in most cases, destroyed. The town's economy had been completely brought to a halt and destroyed, something that would continue throughout the war. Over at the armory grounds, I noticed the Virginia troops had dismantled the machinery to make weapons from the armory buildings. I was told by Israel that the machinery had been crated and was sent to Richmond to manufacture arms for the Virginia state forces.

At the time, several thousand men were assembled at Harpers Ferry, representing nearly all the seceded states east of the Mississippi River. All the forces were under the command of Brigadier-General Joseph E. Johnston. General Johnston had formerly served with the Regular Army, but like many officers, with the commencement of the war he cast his lot with the Southern Confederacy.

My commanding officer was Colonel Thomas Jackson, the former commanding officer at Harpers Ferry before General Johnston's arrival. Colonel Jackson was a native of western Virginia, who had graduated from West Point and served in the war with Mexico. At the beginning of the War of Northern Aggression, he was an instructor at the Virginia Military Institute in Lexington. When I first saw him at Harpers Ferry, his appearance was not military or striking in any particular way. Colonel Jackson wore a plain blue uniform from the Virginia Military Institute, with not a particle of golden lace. His well-worn cadet cap was always tilted over his eyes. The Colonel was mostly quiet and had very little communication with the men. He had a rather sleepy look, and was a very unimposing figure on horseback. As I would discover through my military experiences, Colonel Jackson was a very strict disciplinarian, and he knew how to win battles.

I enlisted with the same company Israel had previously served with, the Floyd Guard. The Floyd Guard was organized after John

Brown's raid. The company took its name from then Secretary of War, John Floyd of Virginia. George Chambers, the owner of the Gault House Saloon and the town's mayor, was the company's captain. The men of the Floyd Guard, who were mostly laborers working in the United States Armory before the war, soon became Company K of the Second Virginia Infantry. The company had been accepted into Confederate service on May 17, 1861. The Second Virginia Infantry was assigned to the First Virginia Brigade, under Colonel Jackson.

The greater part of the companies from the Second Virginia were made up of men from Jefferson County. Five companies in all served in this legendary regiment. They were the Jefferson Guard, Hamtranck Guard, Botts Grays, Letcher Riflemen, and my company, the Floyd Guards. There was one interesting thing about the different companies at Harpers Ferry. They wore different colors and types of uniforms. Company A, the Jefferson Guard from Charlestown, wore dark blue uniforms. The colors were in sharp difference from the gray and yellow of Company B, the Hamtranck Guards from Shepherdstown. Many company members were used to acting and functioning independently. They became angry when their companies became part of the newly formed regiment.

From all Israel shared with me, Colonel Jackson on his arrival at Harpers Ferry in April, disposed of the feather bed and corn stalk militia generals. Changes were rapidly instituted. When I arrived, I became familiar with the officers of the regiment. I recall that most of the officers of the Second Virginia were experienced, well educated, highly disciplined, and well skilled in the theory of war. Colonel James Allen and Lieutenant-Colonel Francis Lackford were classmates at the Virginia Military Institute. Several other officers such as Captains Lawson Botts and Raleigh Colston both attended the Institute. Four other company officers, John W. Rowan, Vincent Butler, William Nelson, and George Chambers, all served in the war with Mexico. I understood these officers had drilled seriously and regularly for over a year.

During the time I was at Harpers Ferry, we drilled at the old armory grounds. The drill was rigorous. Reveille was at 5:00 o'clock every morning. Sometimes we practiced the rudiments of drill and discipline for seventeen hours a day. Often during that time, we spent endless hours marching and counter-marching. One day we marched in a storm of intense hail and rain. It wasn't pleasant and nothing that I was used to doing, but I would soon learn that it was part of being a soldier under "Old Jack." I learned from later experiences why Colonel Jackson placed us under such a heavy burden. This was to steel us up and train us for the endurance we would need in fighting with him as a general of the Second Corps, which he would eventually command in the Army of Northern Virginia.

While at Harpers Ferry, mothers and fathers often visited the camps delivering every imaginable delicacy and fine suits for their sons to wear. Each soldier made himself comfortable. Those that could not adjust to camp life went home. From time to time, Sarah and the boys had the opportunity to visit me at Harpers Ferry. It was a blessing. Often, I looked into her sad eyes, which revealed the uncertainty of an un-chartered future. We could not fool each other. We both knew our army would have the occasion to have a battle with the Yankees. Whether that happened here at Harpers Ferry or some other place was soon to be determined.

On June 14, 1861, we evacuated Harpers Ferry after destroying the Baltimore and Ohio Railroad wooden covered bridge across the Potomac River. Scouting reports had been received by General Johnston that a large Federal army was about to cross the upper Potomac River at Williamsport, Maryland. I later learned the eighteen-thousand-man Federal force was under the command of Major-General Robert Patterson. General Patterson was supposed to keep us occupied in the Shenandoah Valley, but that did not happen.

It grieved me to leave Sarah and the boys. I didn't have time to prepare them or to let them know that the army was departing for some unknown field of battle. I only had time to scribble a few lines on paper and entrust it to Israel to be delivered. It would be some time before I would see Sarah and the boys again.

*Courtesy: Library of Congress*

**Harpers Ferry, Virginia**

## *Chapter Six*

A soldier has many things that go through his mind before going into battle. He thinks of his wife, children, and other family members. I can still recall my first experience the night before going into battle near Manassas. At the time, Private Thomas Arwin and I were good friends since leaving the Ferry. We had marched together and became messmates. Throughout the evening before the Manassas battle, sporadic firing had continued along the picket lines near Bull Run. It makes one think of his own immortality. As we threw a blanket over us, Thomas and I discussed what our fate might bring the next day. On several occasions, the brigade had been formed in line of battle, but they were false alarms. This time we knew there would be a showdown between the two armies. Tomorrow would be a horrible and ugly day, both of us for the first time experiencing the realities of war with all of its wrath and fury.

While I was sleeping, Thomas roused me and made a bargain. If either of us got killed in tomorrow's battle, the other one would see that he was decently buried if our army kept the battlefield. He would also write a correspondence to a family member. It was a practice that continued among friends and messmates by both armies throughout the duration of the war. Since this was the first time I had been approached in this way by another person, it left a feeling of dismay within me. As I learned, it was the way of war. I couldn't sleep the rest of the night after speaking with Thomas.

The fight at Manassas on July 21, 1861, was bloody and savage. The Second Virginia, along with the rest of the First Virginia Brigade, was in the thick of it. Throughout the morning, the Federals had been winning the battle against the Confederate army under Generals Beauregard and Johnston. Our situation looked perilous. Our regiment was placed on the left of the battle line on a ridge known by the locals as Henry's Hill. We waited until waves of bluecoats tasting the fruits of victory, along with their artillery, advanced up the hill toward our battle line. They fired into our ranks causing us to momentarily recoil in confusion. When this happened, Colonel Stuart and his 1st Virginia Cavalry, which had been guarding our left flank, charged down the hill and tore into the Federal's flank. As the Virginia cavalry began their attack, I noticed the Thirty-Third Virginia Infantry also attacking the Federal artillery used to support their infantry. The Thirty-Third Virginia was successful in their attack on the Federal artillery position causing great damage, but was soon counter-attacked by two Federal infantry regiments that were nearby. The Virginians retreated back up the hill beside of our position, creating further confusion among our men.

Our ranks were soon restored to order. The Federals again started up the slope of Henry's Hill. Colonel Jackson watched the Federals advance. Then he ordered the men of the Fourth and Twenty-Seventh Virginia to stand and charge. I can still recall General Jackson's exact words, "Reserve your fire until they come within fifty yards, then fire and give them the bayonet." General Jackson continued, "when you charge, yell like furies."

All of us braced ourselves for the attack. I was nervous, but willing to do my duty. When the signal was given, I jumped to my feet and like the others, I stood, fired and charged like a wild man down the hill. Above the roar of musketry and cannon, the piercing cry that would be forever immortalized as the Rebel Yell, filled the air.

During the charge, all of the regimental organization in the brigade was lost. When we encountered the Federals, we fought hand-to-hand with them. It was the first time that I had inflicted injury on another man, but I was determined that if I did not injure him, then he was going to injure me. This was my first lesson in survival during battle. It was a harsh one because the Federal that I wounded in the chest with my bayonet screamed and cried in such pain and anguish. I do not know if he lived or died. As the fighting continued, some of the men from my regiment managed to drag off one of the Federal cannons. The fighting continued, but we slowly began to push the Federals back down the hill. Soon fresh Confederate troops rushed to our assistance and the day was ours with all of the spoils of war. The Yankees retreated back to Washington City in a panic.

We won the fight because of the obstinate determination that the brigade exhibited. We turned back a number of assaults and refused to yield an inch of Virginia soil. Our losses were high. At Manassas, my regiment lost fifteen dead and fifty-three wounded. The brigade as a whole lost five hundred and sixty-one men. Our spirits had been lifted knowing we had defeated the transgressors and turned them back.

\*\*\*\*

The War of Northern Aggression was like no other conflict this country had ever experienced. Father fought against son, cousin against cousin, friend against friend, and brother against brother. It was no different in my family.

After the fight at first Manassas, I missed Sarah and the boys more than words could describe. I decided to return home, knowing I could be punished for leaving without a pass. I felt victorious and with the win at Manassas, maybe I wouldn't have to return to the army. Maybe there would be a compromise between the Lincoln and Davis governments. But that wasn't to be. I decided to return to the Second Virginia. They were still at Manassas.

The afternoon before returning to Manassas, Owen was fishing along Piney Run. From time to time, Joseph liked to take a break from farming and fish at the stream, especially for evening supper. When Joseph joined Owen, my son informed him of my decision to return to Confederate service. Joseph did not receive the news with joy, but with great misgivings.

Joseph was loyal to the Union just like my brother, Israel. We had family who fought with General George Washington during the revolution against England. Our family had always taken great pride in our national heritage and the sacrifices our ancestors had made through their patriotism. Joseph and Israel believed I was sacrificing my life by serving with the Southern Confederacy.

Joseph came to the house late the same evening and asked to

speak to me alone. I could tell by his expression he was not in a good mood. I understood his feelings. Joseph and I quietly walked out into the front yard where we could be alone.

For about an hour, my brother and I argued our differences over the rights and wrongs of state sovereignty, disunion, and our own individual pride. It was the first time both of us shared our true feelings concerning the conflict. Joseph and I were the most passionate concerning our convictions on any subject among the family. Even though we knew each other's convictions, we had made it a point to keep our differences to ourselves. William, Samuel, and David said little, but I knew they also had their beliefs. I suspected they were Unionist. We all knew with time it would happen that all of us would be forced to choose sides when Virginia seceded from the Union.

Joseph and I resolved nothing from the argument. For Joseph, it was a matter of patriotism for the Union. The rebellion against the Union was wicked and perpetrated by wicked men. Joseph believed that all who followed the lead of these men (including me) were being greatly deceived, and would suffer the consequences for our actions. The one thing we both agreed was that slavery was wrong.

Joseph pledged to assist the Union efforts in any way to put down the insurgency. I was grieved. I tried to understand his convictions. It was hard for me to understand how he could turn his back on his state, his fireside, and his honor as a Virginian. We both went our own way, but with a deeper conviction and determination. The one thing we did come to realize from this meeting was that we were now enemies until this conflict was resolved.

For me it was different. I was fighting for my family, my home, and not so much for the pride of political debate or national patriotism. I wanted to protect my wife and children. I wanted my boys to enjoy all of the liberties and freedoms that God had blessed me with. The reasons that I just gave were not for all. Some of the men I fought with in the Stonewall Brigade viewed the war as a religious crusade. Quite often in the evening or before battle, I read a few verses or chapters in the New Testament. I didn't believe, as some in the brigade did, that death in battle would bring martyrdom. I learned under fire to steel myself for what awaited me and the good Lord would decide my fate.

****

In early spring of '62, while campaigning with General Jackson in the Shenandoah Valley, just before leaving Winchester, I received a correspondence from Sarah. In her correspondence, Sarah mentioned that she had spoken with Israel. Israel told her about the killing of George Rohr, a Unionist from Harpers Ferry and also an acquaintance of mine. George was spying for Colonel John W. Geary of the Twenty- Eighth Pennsylvania Infantry. Colonel Geary's infantry regiment was at Sandy Hook.

Sarah wrote that it all happened on the evening of February 7, 1862, around 7:00 o'clock in the evening, when a flag of truce was displayed in the landing arch in the railroad wall above the ruins of the Harpers Ferry bridge. An unidentified person called for a boat to be sent over. The boat was piloted by a ferryman by the name of Rice with Rohr on board. When they came close to the Virginia shore, the two men were fired on by Confederates under Captain George Baylor. Before the boat could be turned, Rohr was hit by musket fire. He was hit a second time and died from his wounds. Rice threw himself into the Potomac River and managed to keep hidden under the boat. He was nearly frozen to death when he came ashore on the Maryland side of the river.

When shots were fired at Rice and Rohr, the Federal artillery began firing from Maryland Heights. The rebels fled toward Charlestown.

Colonel Geary ordered the buildings at Harpers Ferry, along what we called "The Point", destroyed so that in the future the Confederates couldn't use them for shelter and the Federals would have a direct line of fire from the Maryland shore. The buildings fired upon were the Wager, Galt and Railroad Hotels, the Baltimore and Ohio and the Winchester and Potomac depots, Welch's store, and the telegraph office. Five homes, which were not occupied, were also destroyed. The residences of Mrs. Wager, Mrs. Darton, Mrs. Chambers, George Chambers, our company captain, and William Stevens were also destroyed. It grieved me to hear about this, but such was war.

Sarah also wrote that the town was in shambles and ruins and there were only about a hundred people living in the town. It's sad how a community as prosperous and thriving as Harpers Ferry in such a short time was laid to waste.

Joseph and George Rohr were good friends. I understand from Sarah that when Joseph received the news, he was angry and swore vengeance. I found out much later after the war that my brother had spied for the Union army. He carried valuable information to General Banks concerning our army's movements and the activities of Southern sympathizers in the northwestern Loudoun County region.

I was distressed when receiving the information contained in Sarah's correspondence. I immediately wrote a correspondence to William asking him to watch over Sarah and the boys. I had become very concerned for my family, and thought about desertion, but I cast down those thoughts.

## *Chapter Seven*

All the battles I was engaged in from First Manassas to Chancellorsville appeared to be increasingly more savage, furious, and brutal. There was a determination and desperation with each fight. It was out of a deep conviction that men from the blue and gray fought with such sacrificial bravery, great determination, and unquestionable valor. There is nothing civil about war. The only thing that matters in war is winning and surviving. Many were not that fortunate. One of those was our brigade's commanding officer, General Frank Paxton.

General Paxton was killed on Sunday morning, May 3, 1863. It all happened during the Chancellorsville campaign. Around 6:00 o'clock in the morning, our brigade moved across the Plank Road by the right flank three hundred yards, then by the left flank until we reached a hastily constructed breastwork thrown up by the enemy. Fear gripped the heart of many a good man. I had become separated from my regiment during the movement and was the witness to much confusion. Officers prevailed on the soldiers to move forward, but many refused.

Finally, when we managed to move forward, we became entangled in dense underbrush and swampland. We received volley after volley of musketry from the Federals hidden behind log defenses on good ground. Our men were helpless and fell by the scores. We finally succeeded in freeing ourselves from the obstacles. General Paxton tried to reform the brigade line, but was instantly killed while riding to another part of the line. Afterward, we rushed forward against the Federal lines, fighting for almost an hour before retreating because of Federal reinforcements. The Second Virginia lost sixty-six of its bravest men. Some of those brave comrades I had become close friends with and served with honor.

I had seen enough bloodshed, maiming, and horrifying scenes to last me a lifetime. There was one ghastly scene in particular at Chancellorsville. I can still recall the most horrible sight my eyes ever beheld while serving on a burial detail. On the left of our line, where the Louisiana Brigade had fought the previous evening, they had driven the Yankees through a wooded area and then fell back to their original position. The woods had caught fire from the intense artillery shelling. The scene begs description. I witnessed the dead and wounded from both sides lying where they fell. The fire had burned rapidly. Like many of us, I had heard the screams of the wounded, and felt guilty because I knew I couldn't help. When we went to bury the men, we could see how they attempted to keep the fire from harming them by scratching the leaves away as far as they could reach. They were burned to a crisp. The only way we could tell which side they fought on was when we rolled them over and examined their clothing where they lay close to the ground. There we would find some clothing that had not been burned. We took them and buried them side-by-side in the same grave. It was the most sickening detail I had ever been chosen to serve.

The only dark cloud that hung over the army's victory at Chancellorsville was the loss of General Stonewall Jackson. The Army of Northern Virginia's Second Corps under General Jackson had marched most of the day to outflank and surprise the Federal's Eleventh Corps. We accomplished the surprise and drove them back close to the Chancellor house, which was the headquarters of the Yankee army's commanding officer, Major-General Joseph Hooker. That evening General Jackson went out on reconnaissance with some of his staff. While returning to our lines, he was mistakenly fired upon by men from General Lane's North Carolina brigade. General Jackson suffered several wounds, the most serious of those wounds were to his left arm. Doctor Hunter McGuire, General Jackson's personal physician had no other choice than to amputate his arm.

General Jackson appeared to be recovering after he was moved to Guiney Station, which was about ten miles south of Fredericksburg. But as fate would have it, pneumonia set in and he passed away on the Sabbath of May 10. The army and the whole South mourned his passing. The brigade was terribly shocked with the news of his loss because we believed the general would surely recover. All of us wept like children. He was a great general and leader. Many of the boys said our star of destiny would fade, and that our Cause would be lost without General Jackson. The general was buried in Lexington, Virginia. Since the conclusion of the war, like many from the old Stonewall Brigade, I have visited his grave. I have thought of what might have happened in the war if he would have lived specially to lead us at Gettysburg.

After General Jackson's death, the Army of Northern Virginia was divided into three corps. The First Corps remained under the command of Lieutenant-General James Longstreet. General Lee chose Lieutenant-General Richard Ewell to be General Jackson's successor to command the Second Corps. Lieutenant-General A. P. Hill commanded the new Third Corps.

When General Lee made all preparations, the Army of Northern Virginia began its second invasion of Northern soil. The men were in high spirits and enthusiastic about the possibility that the war would end should we be successful.

What I had witnessed at Chancellorsville was nothing in comparison to the terrible carnage, overwhelming wrath, and great fury of war I witnessed during the third day at Gettysburg.

*Source: Courtesy of Library of Congress*

**Lieutenant-General Thomas (Stonewall) Jackson**

## *Chapter Eight*

In the latter part of May 1863, the Stonewall Brigade was camped at Hamilton's Crossing near Fredericksburg, Virginia. The brigade was under a new commanding officer. His name was Brigadier-General James Alexander Walker, from Augusta County, Virginia. General Walker had attended the Virginia Military Institute.

From all that I knew of General Walker, he was a courageous man that had led his regiment, the 13th Virginia Infantry from Gaines' Mill through the Chancellorsville Campaign. He received his rank to brigadier-general on May 19, 1863. General Walker followed the footsteps of a brave soldier who all of us in the brigade held in high admiration, Brigadier-General Frank Paxton.

About June 1, we received orders to cook three days rations and be prepared to march on a moment's notice. Rations had to be drawn from the Commissary near the Crossing. Some of the companies didn't receive the word in time. Our company was one of those units.

It was late in the evening when twenty of us went to the Commissary to receive our rations. When we arrived, all hands were busy weighing and packing the supplies. We had some time to wait. While waiting, Thomas Arwin and myself noticed a large number of hams lying nearby. No one was guarding them. Hams were reserved for officers and not soldiers of lower rank like Thomas and myself. Ham was something I had not enjoyed since leaving Loudoun County. I looked around to see if anyone was watching me before taking any. Everyone seemed to be occupied. When I gestured to Thomas, we each took several of the hams and hid them. Each of the other soldiers did likewise after we informed them of our noble deed.

When we got back to camp, we had nine hams and our rations, which was bacon. All of the food kept us from hunger for some time. During the war, we never let an opportunity pass without taking extra rations if possible. If we had been caught, the penalty and punishment would have been severe.

Camp life for a Confederate soldier could be trying. Fancy the comforts of such a life as this. We would be roused at dawn and have to crawl out and stand half-dressed in a drenching storm, rain or snow, while the company roll was being called. Afterward, we were allowed to return to our damp blankets.

Sanitation was not the best. Often, I would go down to a marsh to break the ice off a shallow branch or stream, and splash a few handfuls of muddy water onto my face and then wipe it off on the corner of a dirty pocket handkerchief. Afterward, many times I would borrow a broken piece of a comb because I had lost my own. After raking the bits of trash out of my own hair, I devoted the next hour trying to boil a dingy tin-cup of so called coffee. Quite often it was rye coffee, which was a poor substitute for real coffee.

We were not able to steal such luxuries as hams very often. Most of the time, a soldier's fare was made up of a chunk of boiled beef or boiled bacon with cornbread. The meat was tough at best. It was not anything like I had enjoyed at my home with Sarah before the war. How I missed her cooking and her loving smile.

Making a fire was difficult when it had been raining. A soldier would rub the skin off of his knuckles trying to start a fire with green pine poles. After cooking, I would find my hands blackened and grimy with sooty smoke from the snapping, popping, sappy, green pine logs. My eyes were red and my face burned while my back was chilled and still drenched from a pouring rain. Unless there was a crate to sit on, I had to stand to eat. It was rough trying to eat while standing up. Like other soldiers, I took my meat and picked it up with my fingers while eating. It was a matter of satisfying hunger.

I never desired to be in camp for any period of time. The reason was because of the outbreak of disease. Disease did more to reduce the strength of our regiment than bullets or canister. Measles often spread among the men. I was fortunate to some degree because I had the measles when I was a young lad. Outbreaks of dysentery caused a number of deaths in the brigade. It occurred because of unsanitary conditions. All of us worked hard to improve the way we had to live.

One of those ways of better living came through the religious revival held nightly in the various regimental camps. On one occasion, General Jackson's personal pastor, Reverend B. T. Lacy, gave a stirring sermon from the Gospel of John 3:16. The men's hearts were so stirred to righteous living that revival spread through the camps like wildfire. Men began to hand out spiritual tracts and witnessed their faith in Jesus Christ to others. A quiet and deep work had evidently been going on in the hearts of a large number of my comrades.

Revival was not for everyone in camp. I was around dozens of rough, uncouth fellows, whose mingled complaints, playful jokes, unnecessary quarrels, noise and impatience made me sigh at the prospect of spending the entire day and the next under precisely similar circumstances. As war continued, some of these men had second thoughts and made a personal profession of faith in Jesus Christ.

On June 8, the Second Corps under "Old Baldy" Ewell began the march to Culpepper Court House. The Stonewall Brigade was fourth in line. The next day, the brigade camped near Culpepper Court House. We had heard that a cavalry fight had taken place earlier in the day at Brandy Station between Major-General Jeb Stuart and the Yankee cavalry under Major-General Alfred Pleasonton.

Brandy Station was not far from Culpepper Court House. The fighting took place from dawn until late in the day with General Stuart driving the Yankees back across the Rappahannock River. I understood through camp rumor that General Stuart had been surprised by the Yankee general and could have been defeated. The fighting was furious with hand-to-hand conflict. I saw more men that day with saber cuts than any other time during the war. One cavalryman who passed me had a bad wound. His skull was lying bare. I did not think he would live to see the sunrise another day.

That same evening, June 9, we were ordered to prepare three days rations. At the time, none of the foot soldiers really knew what our destination might be. We were soldiers and just followed orders.

I received a correspondence from Sarah before we left Hamilton's Crossing. Sarah informed me that my cousin, Robert Russell, was fighting with the Federal army. Under the light of a glowing campfire, I wrote Sarah a few lines to answer her correspondence. I informed her concerning my welfare and the cavalry fight that took place earlier in the day. Robert fighting for the Yankees troubled me. I asked Sarah to write him and plead with him to return home because I believed the war would soon be over. We would be the victors. The foreign powers would see that the Yankees could never subjugate the South by fighting. I ended by informing her it was not safe to send money to her by mail at this time.

That day was horrible for me because I wanted to be home with Sarah and leave the misery and horrors of war behind. All the men were hoping they would be able to return home to see their wives and family and maybe even spend a night or two with them as long as they were not behind enemy lines. Loudoun County was too far away for me. All the men I spoke with were disappointed. The army was moving too rapidly.

That same day I again played with the thought of taking a French furlough. A French furlough was leaving the army without permission. I knew it could mean severe punishment, but these thoughts tormented my mind every time I heard from Sarah.

## Chapter Nine

When the Federal cavalry chose not to strike again the next day, our division under Major-General Edward "Old Allegheny" Johnson, departed from around Culpepper Court House. General Rhode's division took the lead, with ours following and General Early's division bringing up the rear.

On Wednesday, June 10, our division marched up the Old Richmond Turnpike. This route took us through Sperryville along the Blue Ridge Mountains, and then through Chester Gap to Front Royal. The march carried us through beautiful countryside with rolling pastureland and through patches of woods.

Once we reached the crest of Chester Gap, we paused for a breather. All of us were caked with dust; we were thirsty, and tired. The Shenandoah Valley looked beautiful from on top of the Blue Ridge. Private Thomas Gold said it was "a joy in his heart when from the top of the hill, he at last seen in the distance the long blue hills." In one accord, many in the ranks gave forth a shout of gladness. In honor of returning to the Valley, the Second Virginia and the rest of the brigade was given the honor of taking the advance. All stepped out with renewed vigor and pressed forward.

Once we crossed into the Shenandoah Valley, it was rumored among the ranks that we were heading for Winchester, Virginia. General Johnson had not informed us of our destination. I was glad to be close to home. My hopes were high that I might see Sarah.

The Shenandoah Valley was once a place of tranquility. Before the war, I often visited with my relatives living near Berryville. I can recall when the roadside was dotted with homesteads, farms with dusty, fence-lined roads, fields of wheat and plush pastureland. They were like most people living in the Valley. They owned a farm with a two-story brick home with a steep pitched roof. Their home was surrounded by oak and walnut trees, giving one plenty of shade while sitting on its long porch on a Sunday afternoon after preaching. Cattle and horses roamed freely in the surrounding fields that were covered with thick clover. Pigs, goats, and chickens were plentiful. I can still remember on a Saturday afternoon after a barbecue, we would race our horses across their fields or participate in equestrian tournaments. The Valley was a good place to raise agricultural goods because of its fertile soil. The Shenandoah Valley's apples were the sweetest and juiciest that could be found anywhere.

Now almost two years later, the Valley, like the rest of Northern Virginia, was feeling the fury of civil war. I noticed the toil the war had taken on the Valley. In some areas, fences had been dismantled by soldiers for firewood, and homes were tarnished with neglect because many of the Valley men were in the ranks. Some homes and barns were damaged because they were in the line of artillery fire. The fields were not as plentiful as years past. Still, the Valley was in much better condition than being around Fredericksburg, where the fields were barren and villages such as Fredericksburg were almost destroyed.

All of the men were glad to see the Valley. We were returning home to our loved ones and friends. The first community we entered was Front Royal. The citizens were the first to see us and were very glad for the army's return to the Valley. Many of the citizens knew we were coming because a pontoon bridge had been constructed the previous day. I can still recall the citizens lining the street as we marched through the village. They were wild with jubilation, hoping to see a brother, father, son, or husband. The officers and men responded with equal enthusiasm.

We paused briefly in Front Royal before continuing on to Winchester. "Old Baldy" was in a hurry, so much so that he had us wade the Shenandoah River rather than use the pontoon bridge. I told John Cooper and some of the other men as we forded the river, it was going to be a long night without any rest. After serving with General Jackson, and being so used to flanking marches against the Federals, I believed we would continue toward Winchester. That did not happen. We had already covered about forty miles from Culpepper to Front Royal over mountainous terrain in very hot and dry weather since the afternoon of June 10.

That evening, we camped about five miles north of town. We were informed of our destination. It was another invasion of Northern soil. There was only one troublesome obstacle. There was a Federal force in the area around Winchester that had to be dealt with before we could continue north. The men were ordered to cook three days' rations. I found out later the Federal army with eight thousand men were commanded by Major-General Robert Milroy. General Ewell hoped to capture the Federal division before it could possibly unite with General Hooker's Army of the Potomac.

At 4:00 o'clock the next morning of Saturday, June 13, the brigade moved northwest from Cedarville toward Winchester. Our regiment marched in the advance of the brigade until we came within four miles of Winchester, where we engaged Federal pickets. We continued to drive them back until we came to the junction of Millwood Pike and the Front Royal Road. Here the Federals took up a position behind a stonewall fence. Our boys continued to press them until we drove them from the fence.

The Federals at this time brought up a battery to our front and began to fire on our skirmishers. Soon, Captain J. C. Carpenter's four-gun battery came to our assistance and opened a deadly fire. It was too much for the Federal battery and their infantry support. They began retreating before us.

After the Second Virginia moved to the Millwood Pike, we received a heavy and severe fire of shot and shell from the enemy guns on the heights around Winchester. Around 9:00 o'clock in the evening, the Second regiment rejoined the rest of the brigade. We did very little in the way of fighting. Most of General Early's division advanced on Winchester from the west and fought the battle on that day. Our boys from Louisiana completely routed the Federals, driving them in a full-scale retreat toward Martinsburg and the Potomac River.

My brigade received orders concerning the Federal retreat. At 1:00 o'clock the next morning, the men were up and on the move. We took up a line of march through some fields east in the direction of Berryville. When we came to Shannondale Springs, we headed northwest in the direction of Stephenson's Depot.

Once we arrived, the sound of battle could be heard. My

regiment formed to the right along the country road in line of battle, and immediately advanced toward the Martinsburg Pike. After noticing a body of men moving along the Martinsburg Pike, General Walker attempted to identify them. We could not tell if they were friend or foe. They made no hostile demonstration and refused to answer our calls. When General Walker was satisfied it was retreating Federals, we were ordered to open fire. We fired volley after volley as fast as we could reload our weapons.

The Federals got off a few random volleys. One of those bullets hit me in the left ankle. I fell to the ground and grasped my ankle. I rolled over on my back. I sat up and examined the wound. It didn't appear serious. I thought I must have been struck by a spent shell. As I laid on the ground waiting for help, I noticed the Federals were fleeing. My regiment continued to press them for several hundred yards to a wooded area west of the road. They made no defense and instead hoisted a white flag of surrender.

The Federals who surrendered were from the Fifth Maryland, Twelfth West Virginia, Eighteenth Connecticut, Eighty-Seventh Pennsylvania, One Hundred Twenty- Second and One Hundred Twenty-Third Ohio Infantry regiments. From General Milroy's routed division, our army captured twenty-three pieces of artillery, three hundred wagons with valuable supplies, three hundred horses, and four thousand prisoners. Afterward, I heard through camp rumor that General Milroy had escaped with three hundred of his men. Too bad we did not arrive earlier to try to capture General Milroy with the infantry.

Our cavalry had been operating on our flank and was of no assistance in routing General Milroy's Federals along the Martinsburg Pike. When we took possession of the captured mules and horses, I noticed while waiting on medical attendants and a litter, that some of the men mounted the animals bareback and the best way they could. They were the hardest looking mounted regiment I had ever witnessed, with their knapsacks and blankets around their shoulders; their rifles, no saddles, blind bridles, mounted on the horses and mules. Down the Martinsburg Pike they rode, yelling and shooting, as if it was all a game. They were actually after the large Federal wagon train fleeing along the Martinsburg Pike. They did capture the wagon train.

Many of the men expressed their satisfaction with the way

General Ewell handled the Second Corps. As a matter of fact, they felt General Ewell was the right officer to lead the column in General Jackson's place. All of us were very optimistic.

*Source: Harper's Weekly*

**Winchester, Virginia**

## *Chapter Ten*

I was taken into Winchester to the courthouse along Loudoun Street, which was being used as a hospital. The medical personnel placed me on the porch to await attention from one of the surgeons. While I was waiting, I became very hungry. A young lady of about eighteen arrived and gazed at me. She had a friend with her. I must have been a pitiful sight for her to look upon with my matted bloody trousers, dirty shirt, and grubby appearance lying beside of two groaning forms that wore Federal blue. The two women, who introduced themselves as Kate and Jo, knew as I, the Federals would not see the sun set on the horizon.

Kate took some mush while Jo poured milk from a pitcher into a tin cup and handed it to me. As I was eating, Jo noticed I did not have a pillow or anything else to lay my head on, so she excused herself and returned shortly with a pillowcase and stuffed it with straw. When Kate and Jo were satisfied they could do no more for my comfort, they entered the building to see what assistance they could offer the surgeons.

After about an hour, another much older lady by the name of Mrs. McDonald arrived to be of assistance to the surgeons and the wounded. In my conversation with her, she told me that many of the town's citizens had been up before dawn to greet the Confederate soldiers as they entered town. As a matter a fact, the whole town had turned out and filled the streets. As the infantry columns approached, she said, many of the ladies began to sing in one accord "The Bonnie Blue Flag." The Confederate troops paused until the singing stopped, then they shouted hurrahs, and waved their caps before moving on.

Mrs. McDonald lived on the outskirts of Winchester and was

able to view some of the fighting involving General Early's men. When I asked Mrs. McDonald about yesterday's battle, she said she witnessed troops deploying, skirmishers thrown forward in advance of the main column of infantry, cavalrymen galloping to and fro, and artillery going into battery. As the batteries dueled, one shell passed close to her house and exploded, but fortunately caused no harm or destruction to her property.

About noon there was a lull in the battle. When the fighting did erupt again, cannons began firing, the rattle of musketry was heard, and the fighting was in its full fury. Mrs. McDonald and her children fled for their house. She witnessed General Milroy and his staff ride by her house. General Milroy, she said, appeared agitated and his face was pale in appearance. She was no more than ten feet from him. Crowds of wounded Federal soldiers filled her porch, trying to shelter themselves from the hail of shot and shell. Ambulances arrived with new casualties. She noticed some of the horses drawing the wagons had been wounded, but were continuously pressed into service. As the sun was going down, the fighting ceased. When she went into her backyard after dark, many of the men who had been there earlier had disappeared as well as the ambulances and their wounded horses. Mrs. McDonald's husband was like many of the men living in Winchester. He was serving with the Southern Confederacy. She wondered if she would see him. When she finished talking to me, she went into the hospital.

Several days after arriving at Winchester, I was still not able to return to the Second Virginia, which had been camped near Stephenson's Depot where I was wounded. The surgeon said I was fortunate that my wound was not more serious. All that remained was a very bad bruise above the ankle. It was still very sore and stiff. I would not able to continue the march north toward Martinsburg with my regiment.

The following day, June 16, my division began marching north along the Valley Turnpike. I was greatly disappointed I could not be with them. With nothing to do and only time on my hands, I limped toward the sidewalk along Loudoun Street. I thought doing nothing would hinder my chances of getting better sooner. I still wanted to try and head north and catch up with my regiment as soon as possible.

While sitting on the sidewalk, I noticed Winchester was a very quaint place to live. Many of the shops and taverns along Loudoun Street were made of solid brick. Across from me was the Taylor Hotel where citizens were coming and going, ministering to the wounded. The streets were lined with gaslight lamps to give light by night. The sidewalks were above street level. The citizens of Winchester, from all that I observed, were hard working, very hospitable, and church goers. Before the war, a little over four thousand people called this community their home. Now, the population had dwindled because many of the males were serving with the Confederate army, such as Company F, the Winchester Rifles of my regiment, the Second Virginia Infantry. Other's had just simply gotten their family out of harm's way by moving north or south.

I had already experienced the generosity of the citizens of Winchester. It made no difference if a wounded soldier wore blue or gray, the care was much the same regardless that the town was passionate for the Southern Cause. Thus far in the war, the town had changed hands a number of times between the warring armies. We came close to capturing Winchester once before under General Jackson at the battle of Kernstown. Kernstown was the only defeat that General Jackson suffered. Our forces returned several months later and captured Winchester.

While I was sitting on the sidewalk, an elderly gentleman, who introduced himself as William Jennings, paused near me. We struck up a conversation on life in Winchester before General Ewell and the Confederate army's arrival. Mr. Jennings told me how the town was continuously under martial law during Federal occupation. Federal soldiers often searched homes without notice or regard to personal property, looking for incriminating documents. They also mistreated the residents. The Federals shut them up in their homes and did not allow lights to be burned in their dwellings after 8:00 o'clock in the evening.

According to Mr. Jennings, when the Federals did search homes, the residents were subjected to the most-vile vulgar language and insults they could cast on a person. Whenever they wanted, the Federals looted stores and took whatever they desired without any regard to personal rights. Federal artillery would often take artillery practice by firing wooden artillery cannon balls over the town. Some even hit homes, causing damage and wildly scaring the residents.

One of the most treacherous acts happened in front of some of the ladies living in Winchester. They had witnessed men being shot down in the streets before their very own eyes. It just strengthened their anger and resentment that much deeper against the Federal soldiers.

As Mr. Jennings continued his conversation with me, he said the Federals retreated through the streets of Winchester in May of '62, as General Jackson was pressing the forces under Major-General Nathaniel Banks. The citizens were overjoyed. Townspeople assisted the Confederates by taking potshots at the Federals. One woman leaned out the window of her home and fired on the Yankees and so did a minister. But when it came to ministering to the sick and wounded soldiers, blue or gray, the women of this community assisted as nurses and cooks.

A lady walking along the street recognized Mr. Jennings and paused. Mr. Jennings tipped his hat out of courtesy and said hello. He turned and introduced the lady as Mrs. Mary Greenhow Lee.

When Mr. Jennings and I continued our conversation on life in Winchester and how the citizens were affected by Yankee occupation, Mrs. Mary Greenhow Lee added her experiences. Mrs. Lee said she acted such as other women who would cross the street or step off the sidewalk into the mud to avoid brushing up against Federal soldiers or avoid walking under a U. S. flag. One time a Federal officer approached her on the street, intending to speak to her. As he spoke, she turned her back just as he opened his mouth. Mrs. Lee added that many of the Unionist women of Winchester married Federal soldiers only to discover later they were already married to someone back home.

Mr. Jennings continued the conversation by telling me more of all the sufferings the people of Winchester had endured thus far during the war. He said Major-General Robert Milroy was the worst of the Yankee generals in his behavior and actions against the citizens of Winchester. General Milroy had been in command of Federal forces at Winchester since Christmas Day of '62. Immediately on his arrival, General Milroy required all citizens in Winchester to sign the Oath of Allegiance to the United States as a condition of free movement and other privileges. Some citizens refused to take the Oath of Allegiance. Those citizens were denied the necessities of life such as food and firewood during the cold winter days and nights. There was no mercy extended, not even for those families who had young children living at home.

Another harsh action General Milroy took against the citizens of Winchester was to banish them from the town. Sometimes for little or no reason, he would send citizens through the lines, transporting them by wagon about twenty miles south of Winchester. Sometimes they would be dropped off by the side of the road without food or water during foul weather, even with their children. They were informed not to return to Winchester.

Mr. Jennings said the first family General Milroy banished from Winchester was the Logan family. They were quite wealthy. On the day this harsh act took place, the Logan's two daughters were very ill. It made no difference. General Milroy wanted the house for his headquarters and a residence for his wife to live. As a matter of fact, General Milroy's wife was waiting in a wagon while the Logan's were being evicted from their home.

General Milroy also had buildings dismantled and used the material to construct new forts around the outskirts of Winchester. The residents were left homeless and without a way of making a proper living to provide for their families. The home of Senator James Mason was dismantled brick by brick by the Federal forces. Senator Mason was a diplomat for the Confederate government. He had been involved in the Trent Affair, which almost caused war between the United States and England. The Lincoln government released him and another associate. Senator Mason was not home when this event took place.

Mr. Jennings also told me of another act that was directed at the ladies of Winchester. It occurred when they received the news of General Jackson's death. As was the custom, women wore black to symbolize they were in mourning for a loved one. General Milroy and the Federals were enraged by the ladies' actions and this started a new round of punishment and banishment.

Maybe these harsh actions were only for a location that was militarily important such as Winchester. It was the most important town in the lower Shenandoah Valley. Winchester had six important roads that an army on the move could use to support another fighting force. They led to Pughtown, Martinsburg,

Berryville, Front Royal, Strasburg, and Romney.

When Mr. Jennings and Mrs. Mary Greenhow Lee departed, I pondered about all they had shared with me. I thought of what Sarah and the boys might be experiencing. I wish I knew of their welfare.

## *Chapter Eleven*

By June 19, 1863, General Ewell and the two divisions of Generals Early and Johnson had headed north toward the Potomac River. I was feeling much better and did not want to miss out on what I believed would be the last great battle of the war. Spirits were high in the army and we believed we could defeat the Yankees on a field of battle on any given day.

During the early afternoon of June 20, I examined my ankle. It was still bruised, but I was beginning to feel some relief from the soreness and stiffness. The only Confederate soldiers around Winchester were a few regiments of infantry and the wounded. I did not believe the infantry regiments would be heading north.

While eating breakfast that morning, I heard a rumor among some army surgeons that Major-General George Pickett's division was on the march toward Berryville. I did not know if they would travel to Winchester, so I was determined to find them. Berryville was about ten miles east of Winchester in Clark County. I decided I would walk to Berryville and temporarily join up with the first Virginia regiment I came into contact with until I could rejoin the Second Virginia, which somewhere I believed must be nearing the Potomac River.

Everyone at the hospital was occupied with tending to the more serious wounded when I sneaked away from the courthouse shortly past noon. I say sneaked because I had not been discharged from the hospital by a surgeon. After using a wooded area and passing by the pickets guarding the road to Berryville, I moved along at a slow pace, often pausing to rest and rub my ankle.

About three to four miles outside of Winchester, I came to a stream called Abrahams Creek. As I approached, I noticed another

Confederate soldier drinking from the stream. The soldier turned and noticed I was friendly because I too wore homespun.

The soldier introduced himself as Private William Rogers, Company I, Washington Rifles, Ninth Louisiana Infantry. We sat by the stream for a short period of time talking about home and service. William told me he enlisted in July of 1861. He had taken part in the fighting around Winchester and had injured his arm in the fighting. He too had the same idea as me and was heading for Berryville to march north with the army and rejoin his regiment. One might want to know why William and I would go ten miles out of our way to march north with General Pickett's division. If we had struck out on our own heading north along the Valley Turnpike, we might have been captured by a roaming Yankee patrol from the Harpers Ferry area, or had some Unionist take a potshot at us. Besides, hopefully, Pickett's division would have plenty of rations.

Once William and I returned to the road leading to Berryville, an elderly farmer gave us a ride in his wagon. On the way to Berryville, William and I spoke with the farmer about our lives before the war, our families and about the life of a soldier. The farmer asked about the fighting that took place several days ago around Winchester. After informing him the role the Stonewall Brigade played, William spoke of the Louisianans gallant effort.

According to William, an earthen fort was constructed by the Federals and blocked their way into Winchester. A local guide was sent for and led the Louisiana brigade and the rest of General Early's men in a roundabout way through the countryside so the Federals could not see them. The brigade was moved into a wooded area to rest while Generals Early and Hays crept forward to get a better look at the Federal fort and a smaller fortification. They had succeeded in the element of surprise because the Federal sentries' attention was on some of our men skirmishing near town. General Early was pleased with the distraction.

By 5:00 o'clock in the afternoon, the Louisianans were in position for the attack with twenty pieces of artillery for support. When the artillery opened, the Louisiana brigade inched forth enshrouded by smoke and dust from the artillery. Then they were ordered into a full charge toward the fortifications. The defenders were hardly able to get off a volley of musketry. Once inside of the fortifications, some of the men from another regiment of the Fifth Louisiana turned two artillery pieces around and fired at the fleeing Federals. With the fortifications in Confederate hands, it was difficult for the Federals to hold the larger fort. The Louisianans took advantage of the ample supply of coffee, soup and bread left behind. As for the Federals, they knew they could not hold the larger fort. The Federals evacuated the fort after dark. General Ewell was so impressed with the Louisiana brigade's gallant and heroic part in the victory that he renamed the heights where the fort stood, "Louisiana Ridge."

The elderly gentleman told us he had a son fighting with the Clarke Cavalry. When the war began, they were originally assigned to duty with the First Virginia Cavalry, but later were reassigned as a company to the Sixth Virginia Cavalry. He had not seen his son since the Valley Campaign of '62. He hoped the Sixth Virginia was in the area and that his son might have the opportunity to visit if only for a couple of hours. The farmer's son was named John Bell.

Darkness had settled in. After the farmer dropped us off on the outskirts of Berryville, I noticed the Confederate camps along a hillside, illuminated with many campfires. The scene was very picturesque. Both William and I were very hungry.

When we approached the first picket post, we were escorted to the Sergeant of the Guard because we were looked on as possible deserters. The Sergeant of the Guard was a soldier by the name of Albert Bagley. Sergeant Bagley was from Company B, Danville Grays, Eighteenth Virginia Infantry. At first, he didn't believe our stories. After showing him my ankle, he was convinced and I was allowed to pass the lines for the camp of the Eighth Virginia Infantry. William was further detained by Sergeant Bagley for additional questions why he was not with the Ninth Louisiana. His injury did not impress the Sergeant enough that he should have stayed behind his regiment. I did not question the matter, but moved on.

After the battle at Gettysburg and our army's return to the Shenandoah Valley, I often wondered whatever happened to William. I later discovered his fate from a lieutenant in William's company. One afternoon, the brigades were resting from a hard march along the Valley Turnpike on the retreat from Gettysburg.

While resting and speaking with some of the men, I noticed in the line of march that the flag of the Ninth Louisiana Infantry had been uncased. I walked to where the men were resting and began asking about William. I was referred to one of the officers of his company, Lieutenant James Small. Lieutenant Small said William had fought at Gettysburg and was later wounded at Williamsport during the Confederate army's retreat, where he was believed to have been captured by some of General Custer's men. I grieved for him, knowing he was heading for some prisoner-of-war camp in the North.

To continue my recollections, I went through a number of bivouacs until I came to the camp of the Eighth Virginia. I noticed some soldiers sitting around a glowing campfire eating their supper. I introduced myself to the men who were privates John Atwell, Hector Saunders, Alfred Rollins, and Randolph Shotwell.

Private Saunders offered me some of their rations of salt pork and hard cornbread. It made no difference because I was hungry and willing to eat anything that was going to relieve my hunger. We began a conversation.

After I had told my three new acquaintances all that had happened to me in the fighting I had participated in around Winchester, Private Rollins spoke of the division's willingness to get into a fight. According to Private Saunders, the Eighth Virginia, along with the rest of General Pickett's division, left the Army of Northern Virginia along the Rappahannock River in February and headed south where they finally camped at Chester's Depot. From Chester's Depot, they traveled by railroad to Tarboro, North Carolina. For the next four weeks, the regiment helped to keep the Federals confined at New Bern while the supply wagons crossed the countryside looking and gathering badly needed supplies. It was easy duty and for a while they were away from the killing and maiming of war.

By April, 16, 1863, the regiment received orders and returned to General Longstreet's command near Suffolk, Virginia. While in the area, they continued to help with gathering supplies of bacon and corn. Finally, the Eighth, along with the rest of Pickett's division, headed north through Richmond. It was not without controversy. At first General Pickett had five brigades under his command, but now with the detachment of General's Jenkins and

Corse's brigades, only three Virginia brigades remained. They were under the command of Generals James Kemper, Robert Garnett, and Lewis Armistead.

It was getting late so I spread out a blanket given to me by R. B. Sampson. After borrowing a pencil and paper, I hastily wrote Sarah and informed her of my welfare. Then I lay down and tried to get some sleep, not knowing what tomorrow would bring.

## *Chapter Twelve*

The next morning after I got up, I reported to Captain W. R. Bissell of Company A, Hillsborough Border Guards. Captain Bissell told me he was from Maryland. When the war began, he crossed the Potomac River and enlisted in the Eighth Virginia while they were organizing and drilling at the Leesburg Fairgrounds. The regiment was mustered into Confederate service on May 8,1861. After reorganization took place in the regiment during the winter of 1862, Captain Bissell was elected by the men of his Company to replace Captain Heaton, who was transferred to the Nitre and Mining Bureau. Captain Heaton had commanded Company A since the beginning of the war.

Captain Bissell and I went next to Colonel Eppa Hunton's tent. When I told Colonel Hunton and Captain Bissell about the fight at Winchester and showed them my still bruised ankle, I received their consent to march with them toward the Potomac River as long as I could keep up. There would be no straggling in the ranks. Then I was expected to rejoin the Second Virginia at the first opportunity.

Colonel Hunton wanted to know where I was from. I told him Loudoun County, Virginia. Then Colonel Hunton wanted to know what my vocation was before the war. I told him I was a farmer. He said he was from Brentsville in Prince William County and before the war, he had practiced law. He also made it known to me that he was a faithful democrat and had served as a delegate to the Virginia Secession Convention as an "Immediate Secession Candidate." When Virginia seceded from the Union, he immediately applied for a commission in the Virginia state forces.

On the way back to the Company's bivouac area, Captain

Bissell told me the Eighth Virginia was a fighting regiment that had seen hard service since the beginning of the war. From Manassas to Fredericksburg, they had served with honor. At Ball's Bluff along the Potomac in Loudoun County, the regiment had suffered dearly in casualties. They were commanded to charge an artillery battery. The battery proved to be troublesome. Two Mississippi infantry regiments also joined in the assault against the batteries. This caused a panic among the Federal forces, driving them into the Potomac River with great loss.

Because of the Eighth regiment's gallantry, General Beauregard's wife made a flag for them from one of her own silk dresses. On June 27, 1862, at a place called Gaines' Mill, the Eighth suffered their greatest loss thus far in the war. In September 1862 at Sharpsburg, along Antietam Creek, there were only twenty-two men in the ranks to help beat off General Burnside's attempt to crush the Confederate right flank. Eleven of those men became casualties. I was impressed with the regiment's record of service, and their dedication to a Cause they believed in. They were Virginians whose honor was their word.

On this same day, Sunday, June 21, I did not get to attend preaching. Instead, we received orders to march from Berryville to Snicker's Gap. Federal cavalry was trying to break through General Stuart's cavalry screen along the Blue Ridge Mountain. Our army was scattered throughout the Valley from Winchester to the Potomac River. If General Hooker and the Federal army discovered our intentions, they could have attacked and defeated us. I believed we would see battle because it was rumored through the ranks that Federal infantry supported their cavalry. I tried not to reveal in my walking that I was still experiencing some soreness with my ankle. I wanted to serve and be a part of protecting my liberties, my fireside, and most of all, my family.

While on the march toward the Shenandoah River and to the mountain gap, I momentarily had to fall out of rank and tie my brogan shoe. When I fell back into rank, I marched alongside of Private Shotwell. In our conversation, he remarked about the difference in weather today from earlier in the week. When the division marched north, Private Shotwell said it was so hot that it was very difficult for men just out of winter quarters. In winter quarters men were well screened from the sun. They were not quite used to marching under such oppressive conditions caused by the hot sun. On the march to Berryville, he witnessed men dropping out of the ranks because of fatigue, gasping for air, and some were even dying or already lying along the road, dead.

Private Shotwell continued his recollections. All of the men in the regiment found the dust intolerable and suffocating. The dust was like a powder that filled the air like smoke. It filled his hair, nostrils, eyes, and skin until it became very unbearable. His clothing was wet with perspiration from wearing his accouterments, canteen, and blanket. The dust mixed with the perspiration formed a paste on his skin and clothing. I knew what he was saying. I had been on enough force marches through Virginia under General Jackson and witnessed the scenes played out on many occasions. As I looked around the ranks, the men appeared tired. Their faces were covered with beards and tanned by the hot sun. Young boys in their teens looked like middle-aged men. War had a trying effect on us all.

When we arrived along the Shenandoah River, I removed my brogans and accouterments, and placed my weapon over my head. I found the river to be cold. After fording the river, we marched quickly up the mountain to the crest. I was posted as a guard. We stayed there for a while. The cavalry was constantly coming to and fro, skirmishing with the enemy. We cheered them on. During that time, I came to a greater appreciation for the cavalry because they had not only fought the battle at Brandy Station on their own, but now they were facing the same opposition and keeping them away from the mountain gap without the infantry's assistance.

From the crest of Snicker's Gap, the view was beyond description. As the slanting rays of the setting sun settled on the western horizon, I stood there looking across miles upon miles of the Shenandoah Valley. It was a peaceful sight that caused me for a moment to forget the anger and horrors of war.

Our regiment bedded down for the night. The next morning the Federal cavalry threat had ended. It was raining, breaking the dry spell. It was feared among the commanding officers that the Shenandoah River might flood and the infantry would be unable to pass over the swollen river. We departed from the mountain's crest. Again, I had to remove my brogans and equipment and wade the river, which was high, but passable.

On the way back to Berryville, I noticed a flashy-looking officer at the head of the column with a riding whip in his hand. When I asked Private Randolph Shotwell, he told me it was Major-General George Pickett. General Pickett had long hair, which he wore in ringlets resting on his shoulders. Private Alfred Rollins, who was marching beside me, said the general kept his hair trimmed and highly perfumed. Private Rollins added that General Pickett's beard was also curly and gave out the scents of Araby. They both described him as a dashing individual who sometimes would be given over to his temper.

Private Shotwell commented that General Pickett came from a Virginia aristocratic family. The general graduated from the United States Military Academy at West Point, New York in 1846. He graduated with several other noble generals of the war such as George B. McClellan and Thomas "Stonewall" Jackson. General Pickett had actually commanded the brigade that the Eighth Virginia was part of until he was wounded in the shoulder at Gaines' Mill. Afterward, Brigadier-General Robert Garnett assumed the leadership of the brigade. When General Pickett returned to service, he was promoted to the rank of major general. His promotion was effective on October 10, 1862.

Private Shotwell spoke of an incident during the early spring of 1862 that personally involved him. He said that General Pickett wanted to inspect the regiments of his brigade. The general had singled out Private Shotwell and wanted to inspect his musket. He put on a clean white glove and ran the finger across the barrel, only to find a rusty streak on his clean glove. Colonel Hunton tried to intervene on Private Shotwell's behalf, but the general took out his handkerchief, blew his nose, and turned away without speaking a word to Private Shotwell. Private Shotwell added the experience was very mortifying to him.

Under General Pickett's leadership the division had not yet been committed to battle. The next would be his first. The men were anxious to see how they would be tested under his leadership. My impression of General Pickett was he looked like a serious character.

## *Chapter Thirteen*

On June 25, 1863, General Pickett's division of about five thousand eight hundred men came upon the Potomac River near Williamsport, Maryland. According to my timepiece, it was 2:30 in the afternoon. When I stepped into the river, I found it was very easy for us to ford. It was only two and one-half feet in the deepest part of the river. When my regiment stepped on the Maryland shore, one of our bands was playing patriotic airs. Thousands of rough voices in the ranks joined in the singing. As I looked around the area, I was very surprised to see men, women, and Negroes of all ages silently watching us from the high ground near the river.

We marched on a few more miles until we came to Hagerstown where the brigade paused just north of the town. My new brigade under General Robert Garnett was formed up to witness an execution. The soldier was from the Fifty-Sixth Virginia Infantry. He was Private John E. Riley. Private Riley had repeatedly sold himself as a substitute and then deserted. For your understanding, a substitute was a person that received money from someone who had been drafted into service. The substitute would take that person's place and they would not be called upon to serve. This particular individual had gotten caught substituting numerous times and now had to pay the extreme penalty for his crimes.

It was raining when the brigade formed ranks around the condemned soldier, who was standing in an open field. His hands were tied behind his back and he was blindfolded. He was made to kneel before an open, crudely made wooden coffin. One of the bands began playing the funeral dirge. Twelve men were selected to be the firing squad. The muskets of one-half of the men on the firing squad contained musket balls, while the other half fired nothing but powder. This was so the soldiers making up the firing squad would not know who fired live ammunition. I will never forget the moment when the officer gave the command and the crackle of musketry broke forth. The condemned man slumped over and died. He was an example to all of us of the severe consequences of desertion.

At Hagerstown we camped for the evening. We were given a whiskey ration. Such rations were not unusual to give to soldiers when they suffered unusual labor or exposure to the harsh weather. It was looked upon as helping a soldier's health. Sometimes it was looked upon because an army had invaded its enemy's territory and would win a great victory.

The soldiers were lively when they gathered around fires made from Northern farmers' fence rails. I did not drink my whiskey, but gave my ration to Private Hector Saunders. I noticed we were not the only regiment enjoying the whiskey ration. Other regiments in the brigade were doing likewise. Some of the soldiers had a little too much to drink and were feeling the effects of the whiskey. Spirits were high and the men spent time joking and enjoying some horseplay. I thought of how good it was to be able, for a short period of time, to take my mind off of the emotional effects of the war.

The Eighth Virginia was brigaded with four other Virginia regiments. They were the Eighteenth, Nineteenth, Twenty-Eighth and Fifty-Sixth regiments of infantry. Our brigade strength was one thousand two hundred and eighty-seven men. We were under the command of Brigadier-General Richard Garnett.

In 1862, I served under General Garnett when he was the commanding officer of the Stonewall Brigade. He succeeded General Jackson when he was promoted to the rank of major general. General Garnett was from Essex County, Virginia. He attended the United States Military Academy at West Point and became good friends with Brigadier-General Lewis Armistead. Before the War of Northern Aggression, General Garnett served with the Sixth United States Cavalry and had fought against the Seminole Indians in Florida.

Generals Jackson and Garnett did not get along very well with each other. Their differences came to a showdown during the battle of Kernstown. General Garnett called for a retreat without "Old

Jack's" permission, causing us to surrender the field to the Federals. It all happened while the Stonewall Brigade was fighting along a stone fence not too far from the Pritchard house. Many of us were out of ammunition and were about to be over run by the Federals. General Garnett was in the middle of the fighting. He had no other choice but to order us to retreat. If he had not, then our center would have given way and many of us would have been captured. For his actions, General Jackson pressed charges against him.

Quite a few witnesses testified in General Garnett's behalf during the court- martial proceedings. Finally, General Jackson was pressured by the court overseeing the proceedings to drop the charges against him. General Jackson agreed, but refused to allow General Garnett to serve under his command. General Lee knew General Garnett was a good soldier and a good leader, and gave him command of General Pickett's old brigade. General Garnett always had the best interest of the men of the Stonewall Brigade at heart and he fully enjoyed their trust and respect. It was no different in this brigade.

I don't think General Garnett ever got over the incident with General Jackson because I had overheard, while in camp, officers of the Stonewall Brigade remarking that he continued to brood over the incident. He considered it an insult on his character. He was emotionally bruised by the accusations brought against him by General Jackson.

General Garnett suffered an accident while crossing the Shenandoah River at Snicker's Gap on June 20. A horse kicked him on the lower leg, causing a painful bruise. The general was forced to ride in an ambulance because of his injury. Since Colonel Hunton was the senior officer of the brigade, he temporarily took charge.

On the outskirts of Hagerstown, there was heavy traffic as wagons, and droves of cattle and sheep from the farms in Pennsylvania were being sent to the rear. Hagerstown was not a town of Southern passion. I came to this conclusion based on the fact that as we passed through, all houses were shuttered and, in most cases, abandoned. The citizens who did stand on the streets, I noticed, stared at us with resentful expressions and indifference. Still, there were a few friendly folks. There were some Southern sympathizers living in Hagerstown because the next morning, when we departed north for Greencastle, Pennsylvania, I noticed some "Bonnie Blue Flags" waving from a few windows.

When we crossed the Mason Dixon line, which we knew by a little stone marker along the road, into Pennsylvania, the column broke into hurrahs and even gave some Rebel Yells. The nearest spring was a distance from where we paused. Many of the men just fell down where they were, pulled their caps down over their faces and took the time to rest. Some ate hardtack. Hardtack is a hard cracker that's as tough as shoe leather and is salty. It does a lot to make one thirsty. Most times, we put it in coffee or water to soften it. If soldiers had beef or rusty bacon, they quietly ate it.

I ate a small piece of hardtack. As I looked around the countryside, I was impressed with the rich Pennsylvania farmland. While the brigade was resting along the roadside, I examined some of the soil and found it to be rich and fertile. These farmers were blessed. Looking across the fields, they were lush and rich in wheat, clover and corn. The barns were huge, built of brick or stone. They dotted the countryside everywhere the eye could see.

The one thing missing from the farms were horses, cows, chickens and pigs. I knew the farmers, upon learning of our army's invasion of their state, hid or took their herds out of harm's way. We had already received orders from General Lee that plundering would not be tolerated and private property and civilians would be left unharmed. Still, an abnormal amount of chicken and fresh meat was being cooked around the campfires at night.

Straggling by soldiers in the brigade was forbidden. Officers kept the men moving closely in rank. While along the roadside, I spoke with an officer of the Eighteenth Virginia Infantry by the name of William Miller. Lieutenant Miller did not agree with General Lee's order forbidding the destruction of civilian personal property. He told me Pennsylvania was one large field of wheat and there was no danger of starving out these wretches. He believed our army should do all the injury that we could do to pay back the Federals for what they had done to our country.

When General Pickett's division arrived in Greencastle, I found the town to be neat and pleasant. Maybe one thousand five hundred to two thousand citizens called the community their home. When we arrived, we found the stores and houses closed and shuttered. Very few men appeared, but a large number of ladies lined the streets. Our bands serenaded the ladies to the music of "The Bonnie Blue Flag," "Maryland, My Maryland," and "Her Bright Smile Haunts Me Still."

The men kept step to the music and appeared very joyful. I remembered seeing a little girl standing on a vine covered porch beneath blue morning glories. We lifted our hats to her and I noticed General Pickett did likewise. She called us traitors. We laughed. We knew our kids did the same thing when the Yankee army passed through our towns and villages in Virginia.

Our division moved on. At sunset, men began to straggle and faces were filled with pain. Everyone was hot and hungry. Uniforms were wet with perspiration. Off in the distance, I saw campfires burning. It was the infantry advance of our division. One of General Pickett's aides arrived informing us to camp near the big spring. Our brigade was ordered to be prepared to march again at 6:00 o'clock the next morning.

I figured our brigade must have marched at least thirty miles on that day. Like many of the men in the brigade, my feet were sore, I was weary, and hungry. I decided just to lay along the road in my wet coat and trousers. I did not even have supper. My closing thoughts for the day were that soldiering was not fun and was not a desirable vocation.

## *Chapter Fourteen*

On the morning of June 27, I discovered that our men had slept in fields, barns, and haystacks. A number of men were around fires they had built alongside of the road, cooking what few rations were left. The division began moving toward Chambersburg. Chambersburg was about eleven miles north of Greencastle. The march to Chambersburg was uneventful. We passed through several small communities unworthy of notice. It was dusty and, hot and I was again very weary when we pitched camp about one mile north of Chambersburg.

Our camp was in a shady grove. It was peaceful. There was not a ripple of excitement crossing the camp with the exception that roll call was held four times a day. Roll call helped to keep down the straggling among the ranks. We were not allowed in town without a pass and even when we did go into Chambersburg, we could not disturb anything. Several times when I did go into town, I went to a house and knocked on the door looking for something to eat. Most of the time, the citizens obliged. I thought they did this mostly out of fear.

At one of the homes in Chambersburg, I was informed by the gentleman of the house that he had heard General McClellan was in Harrisburg with a Regular and militia force of sixty thousand men, ready to march on us and defeat our army. I laughed, not taking him seriously. While at Chambersburg, I took the opportunity to bathe and wash my clothing. What was left of them was ragged. I was embarrassed. But rags were better than being naked, which I was close to being.

Chambersburg was a town with nice well-built homes and various factories. The homes were neat and conveniently built with no elegant style to them. The country around Chambersburg was beautiful and well cultivated. It was some of the best country we had traveled through since moving north of the Potomac River. The eastern side of the town was handsomely laid out with a number of beautiful residences. The citizens did well for themselves.

I noticed all around me the citizens were indifferent and really did not care one way or the other, as long as we left them alone. I believed many of the residents were of strong backbone and very loyal to the Union. Of course, the town was under martial law since we occupied enemy territory, and no citizen of Chambersburg was allowed to leave the town. Now they knew what it was like to experience some of the oppressions of war such as our families had experienced in Virginia.

We still could not plunder so while some officers paid as much as fifty cents for a meal at one of the Chambersburg hotels, I mostly went to one of the nearby farms to forage. I found the farmers most cooperative to sell their eggs and coffee, but I had to pay the price they desired. I had Confederate scrip, but they would not accept it. Instead, I had a few greenbacks I had stolen from a wounded soldier at Winchester, who I did not feel would have the need for his money anymore.

While the Army of Northern Virginia was moving freely around the north and east of Chambersburg, word was spread through the camp that General Pemberton had defeated General Grant and his Federal army at Vicksburg. Word also arrived that General Ewell and some of our ragtag army had advanced as far north as Carlisle Barracks. Carlisle Barracks was not too far from the Susquehanna River and the Pennsylvania capital of Harrisburg. For now, I thought, our boys were really living in comfort.

Many in the ranks believed victory and Southern independence was near. If we defeated the Army of the Potomac, then the war would end because Abraham Lincoln would be forced by the Copperheads of the North to negotiate peace with President Davis and the Southern Confederacy. I was optimistic because this meant I could return home to Sarah and the family, picking up the pieces of my life once more.

We were left to guard the army's wagon trains until Brigadier-General John Imboden's cavalry brigade returned from a raid somewhere in western Maryland. Over the next three days, we were busy under Major Edmund Berkeley destroying the Cumberland Valley Railroad buildings, workshops, and machinery. We used heavy iron rails to punch holes in the buildings. Some of the men of our regiment from Haymarket, Virginia shouted "Remember Haymarket." This was because of the destruction the Virginia village suffered the previous year at the hands of General Pope's Federal army. We joined in with the Fifty-Third Virginia to destroy the railroad track. It was hard labor. We took wooden cross-ties, heated the iron rails in the flames and then wrapped the lengths of glowing hot metal around trees.

One piece of railroad equipment did give us a difficult time. It was the railroad's turntable used to turn locomotives around in a different direction. We had tried a number of times to destroy the turntable, but were unsuccessful. Finally, cordwood was used to build a fire on it. Then as it cooled it warped and cracked the turntable.

As we went about the task of destruction, all the men spoke freely of fighting the Yankees before too many more days passed. During this time, I often thought of Sarah and the boys. By now, they knew our army had crossed the Potomac River and were invading Northern soil. Somewhere in my heart, I knew this was going to be a furious fight. My reasoning was the Yankees would be fighting on their soil and defending their wives, children, and families. Now with our invasion of their soil, they must know how we felt about them invading our soil, homes, and causing destruction of our personal property.

Religious revival spread once more throughout the army. I witnessed many men surrendering their lives to the Lord Jesus Christ. And again, as in the past when they knew they were going into a desperate battle with the Federals, they gave up card playing, cursing, and drinking whiskey. Instead, they began to read their Testaments. A soldier never knew when he might draw his last breath in this world. It was best to be prepared when the time came.

A courier arrived late in the afternoon at General Pickett's headquarters. The rumor quickly spread throughout the camp that General Joseph Hooker was no longer the commanding officer of the Army of the Potomac. Major-General George Meade of the army's Fifth Corps had replaced General Hooker at Frederick, Maryland. This told me the Army of the Potomac was in Maryland and in full movement toward Pennsylvania.

****

Shortly after 2:00 o'clock on the morning of July 2, 1863, a courier arrived at General Pickett's headquarters with orders from General Lee to bring the division immediately to Gettysburg. We cooked a quick breakfast. Without a complaint, the men fell into line full of optimism and confidence knowing we would defeat the Army of the Potomac, even with their new commanding officer, George Meade.

A few miles from the crest of South Mountain and the Cashtown Gap, my brigade passed the burned-out ruins of the Caledonia Iron Works. The men shouted hurrahs. A radical Republican congressman, Thaddeus Stevens, owned the Caledonia Iron Works. Thaddeus Stevens was chairman of the House Ways and Means Committee. I knew of his fame before the war. He was an abolitionist, and was active in the Underground Railroad. He was also a great supporter of President Lincoln and emancipation as a way to weaken our Cause.

When my brigade reached the crest of South Mountain, we were informed of the first day's fighting at Gettysburg. From all that I learned from a courier who had been at Gettysburg, General Henry Heth's division of General A. P. Hill's Third Corps was the first to see battle. They had engaged Federal cavalry near the town. The Federal cavalry, I found out later, was under the command of Brigadier-General John Buford. It took some time to get our men into a battle line. The Yankees knew it because they were only fighting a delaying action until their infantry of the First and Eleventh Corps, who were marching from Emmitsburg, Maryland arrived.

General Hill continued to throw in additional divisions as the Yankees of the First and Eleventh Corps arrived on the battlefield. Many were killed and wounded on both sides. The day was finally decided in our favor when General Ewell and the Second Corps of our army arrived from the north of Gettysburg. With Generals Ewell and Hill attacking from north to west, the Federals were driven back through the streets of Gettysburg to a ridge south of town. The ridge was known as Cemetery Ridge. Our men took as many as four thousand prisoners on the first day of fighting at Gettysburg.

I did give thought to how my comrades of the old Stonewall Brigade faired in the fight. I missed serving with them. I thought of my friends and if they survived.

After an hour on the mountain, our division continued toward Gettysburg along the Chambersburg Pike. We were still about five miles from Gettysburg when the division came to a halt. We were told to camp near a stone bridge. We were exhausted, being twelve hours on the march, covering about twenty-three miles. Off in the far distance, I heard the muffled booming of cannons. All of us knew a desperate fight was taking place. Hopefully, we were getting the better end of the battle.

General Longstreet did not call us into the fight because he had been informed by General Pickett's aide, Captain Robert Bright, that we had executed a force march and were tired. Captain Bright informed General Longstreet we could fight for an hour or two, but not any longer. General Longstreet decided on that day not to use us, but would allow us to rest. Later that evening in camp, I learned from Private Robert Rogers, who had carried a message from Colonel Hunton to General Pickett that Captain Bright had returned to General Pickett's headquarters with verbal orders from General Longstreet. General Longstreet said he would have work for General Pickett and our division tomorrow.

With the news General Longstreet had delivered to General Pickett, I knew the division would be engaged tomorrow. As I glanced around young somber and joyful expressions, I wondered how many of them would survive the desperate fighting that was surely to come tomorrow. All soldiers think of their fate during times such as this.

I went off by myself and found a quiet place along Marsh Creek and thought of Sarah and the boys. I didn't know if I would see them again. I wept. Never before in my war experiences did I feel this strongly before entering a battle. I turned and pulled Sarah's photograph from my pocket and had enough light from a nearby campfire to look on her face. As I held her photograph close to my chest, I wanted to be home, not in some far away place like

Gettysburg. When I returned her photograph to my haversack, I walked over to the campfire where several other soldiers of the Eighth Virginia were seated. I pulled out my Testament. I began reading in Second Corinthians, Chapter 12, verse 9. I read "My grace is sufficient for thee: for my strength is made perfect in weakness." I found comfort in those words.

From the conversation among the men of my regiment, we were the only division that had not seen service at Gettysburg. I knew that was about to change. Many in my regiment would pay the cost of freedom with the sacrifice of
their lives at **Gettysburg: The Field of Glory**

*Source Harper's Weekly*

**Confederates army at Chambersburg, Pennsylvania**

## *Chapter Fifteen*

I was awakened by a bugle call. It was still dark when I pulled out my timepiece to see what time it was. It was 3:00 o'clock in the morning. I was stiff and sore from the march of the previous day. As we fell in for roll call, the flags hung limp in the morning air. Some of the men joked while others were somber. After roll call and a small piece of hard bread, we were soon on the march again.

Major James Dearing and his artillery battalion had already departed before us. It was still under the cover of darkness when it came time for us to begin marching toward the battlefield. General Kemper's brigade took the lead. Our brigade under General Garnett followed, with General Armistead's bringing up the rear of the division. This order of march would have some influence on the placement of each brigade for the battle we all knew would come sometime during the day.

Sarah and the boys were already in my thoughts. Unlike other battles I had taken part in, this one for some reason frightened me. I did not know if this was a premonition of death. Since crossing the Potomac River, I had not received a correspondence from Sarah and I was unable to send her one. She must be worried, I thought, especially by now with knowledge of the first day's fighting at Gettysburg.

After marching a short distance, we halted for some time while being issued twenty additional cartridges. This made sixty in all. For some reason, I knew our division would be involved in the thick of the day's fight. Bloody work was surely ahead of us.

Our division finally came to a by road known by the locals as the Knoxlyn Road. General Robert E. Lee sat motionlessly on his horse and quietly watched us pass. When I look back on this moment that is so vivid in my mind, I believe General Lee as he looked on us, knew the fate of the Confederacy hung on the fifteen Virginia regiments that made up the three brigades of General Pickett's division.

We had a guide sent to us by Lieutenant-Colonel Moxley Sorrels of General Longstreet's staff. They wanted to disguise the division's intentions and movements from the Federal's signal station around Gettysburg. The guide rode at the front of the column with General Pickett.

The division took another by road, heading east once more. On a road known by the locals as the Hereter's Mill Road, the column moved along with no sense of urgency. Some men in the ranks talked of home and family. This often happened among the enlisted soldier when they knew they were going to go into a battle. The division continued until we angled off southeast, crossing the road to Hagerstown.

We soon came to a wooded area where we paused to rest. The division moved on toward a field near a small stream known as Pitzer's Run. While at Pitzer's Run I took a drink of its cool water and then filled my canteen. As I was doing so, I noticed surgeons and medical attendants beginning to set up field hospitals in some nearby homes and a mill known as Bream's. It was a good location since it was in a dell in a grove at the rear of the troops. There was a large orchard nearby and an ample supply of apple butter pots. Medical attendants began filling them with water and also began setting up makeshift operating tables. From what I have seen during the war, hospitals were places of suffering. They were for the most severely wounded, and nothing but terrible death holes. Off in the distance, I could now hear the muffled roaring sound of artillery fire. I knew the fight had begun.

I looked around and noticed the four Presgrave brothers (John, George, William, and James) of my regiment talking. What was so particular about the Presgrave brothers was that they all were over six feet tall. I was only five foot seven inches tall, about the normal height of most soldiers. The Presgrave brothers were strong looking men, but men as tall as they were made good targets to shoot at. I prayed for their safety and that they would survive the coming conflict. They were not the only brothers in the regiment, there were also the Berkeley and Lunceford brothers, who took part in the deadly struggle on the third day at Gettysburg.

After about twenty minutes, we were ordered into line, only this time we changed from column to double-ranked battle formation. Captains were in the front and lieutenants and sergeants were on each side as file closers. Our brigade was on the extreme right. It was at this time that I noticed General Garnett. He was still suffering from his injury.

The division continued on, still hidden from the Federal's observation. I noticed some of the devastation and carnage of the first day's fight. There still remained on the field blackened and bloated bodies. I could smell the stench from not only their bodies, but those of horses that had been killed. I wanted to get the scenes out of my mind as soon as possible. Again, we were ordered to halt behind another lower lying wooded ridge where we went through inspection of our weapons by our officers. Our battle flags were furled once more.

I looked around and noticed preparations were taking place among the artillerymen. Ammunition wagons were nearby and artillerists were busy transferring ordnance from those wagons into their caissons and limbers. There appeared to be expressions of determination on each face. I have known these expressions before at such places as Second Manassas, Fredericksburg, and Chancellorsville. It usually meant serious work still lay ahead. I looked at the men around me and wondered for a moment how many of us would survive whatever the army's high command had planned for this day.

I overheard one teamster speaking with an artilleryman about the previous day's fight. The artilleryman said the fight had taken a frightful toll on our army. It had cost us the services of General William Barksdale and General Paul Semmes while leading their brigades. Both were severely wounded and eventually died. The artilleryman said he heard Captain Lamar of General McLaws' staff say to another officer that he watched General Barksdale at the head of his men. During a crucial period in the fighting, General Barksdale had removed his hat with his long white hair blowing in the breeze, exhorting his men to follow him forward. He was shot down by the Yankees.

I heard the names of places from the second day's fighting from the artilleryman such as the Round Tops, the Wheatfield, and the Peach Orchard that belonged to the Sherfy family. All were places men from the blue and gray were dead or dying from fighting. The artilleryman was confident that had General Longstreet and General Ewell sufficiently coordinated their assaults, our forces would have beaten General Meade and his army before sunset. In the attack, our men had almost destroyed General Sickle's Federal Army's Third Corps. If it had happened such, as the artilleryman had believed, then maybe we would not have been fighting on the third day. Maybe the battle would have concluded with us being the victors. That was not to be. All of us veterans knew the signs. Another struggle lay in front of us and more lives would be lost before the end.

Source: Author's Collection

**Gettysburg, Pennsylvania**

## Chapter Sixteen

At the wooded ridge known as Spangler's Woods, our men began to settle down. The ridge was a reasonable place because it was steep. We believed it would continue to keep us from Federal observation. We were all hungry. I pulled out a corn dogger. A corn dogger is corn meal and flour mixed in bacon grease with enough hot water to make the dough stiff. After patting it into the size of a silver dollar, it is fried until crunchy. While eating the corn dogger, I watched while some of the others pulled out their pieces of bacon to make a frugal meal. For some of them, I knew it would be their last meager meal on this earth. Many were in silent reflection as they ate.

As I was eating, I listened to the birds chirp and gazed at the many winged insects flying around. Wild flowers and the cultivated grain of the fields were in their beauty and fruitage. The trees lifted and waved their leafy branches in the life-giving air. Never was the sky or earth more serene, more harmonious, and more aglow with light and life. In blurring discord with it all was man alone. Thousands and tens of thousands of men, once happy countrymen, now in arms, had gathered in hostile hosts and in hostile confronting lines. As I continued to look around I noticed some of my other comrades, such as Private Hector Saunders, laying on a blanket on the gravelly hillside, taking a nap. Everyone was in a dull and lazy mood waiting for orders, whatever they might be. It felt like it was going to be a hot and oppressive day.

After eating, I climbed to the top of what was known as Seminary Ridge. I noticed, about fifty yards to our front, that our artillery guns were lined up to the left and right of our division as far as the eye could see. Behind the guns were lines of limbers and caissons that had just been filled with artillery shells. They were facing Cemetery Ridge. There must have been a hundred or more cannons. There were more than I had seen thus far in battery at any one battle.

The artilleryman that I had listened to earlier as he spoke with the teamster about the second day's fighting, was now examining the tube of his artillery piece or as we called them, Dogs of War. Other artillerymen were milling about while some were looking in the ammunition chest to make sure they had everything that was needed. I noticed the drivers of the guns were digging holes about six feet long by two feet deep behind the caissons.

I turned and looked in the direction of Cemetery Ridge, which I had learned was the center of the Army of the Potomac. It was sobering for me to realize that a frontal assault, which I had perceived with the artillery alignment, would be costly for our army. I knew now why I had felt such anxiety earlier today. We would cross the field under what would surely be heavy artillery fire from Cemetery Ridge.

Once we were about two hundred yards away from the stone fence along Cemetery Ridge, we would have to scale a high stake-and-rider fence across the road, known as the Emmitsburg Road. The Emmitsburg Road hugs the base of Cemetery Ridge for the first mile or more then diverges into the middle of the valley created by both ridges. At this point, the brigade organization and alignments would be compromised and become disorganized.

We would be exposed to canister fire from the Federal artillery along the stone fence. Canister was three to four dozen one-inch slugs packed in sawdust in a tin cylinder. It was fired from a cannon and had the effect of a shotgun, causing terrible damage to a line of infantry at two hundred yards.

I estimated, as I continued to look at Cemetery Ridge, that it was about one mile between the two ridges. We would be in open field the whole time. It reminded me of the assault the Federals had attempted against our army at the stone fence at Fredericksburg seven months ago.

By now, I had enough experience regarding war. General Lee must have thought the Federal center was the weakest section of their defenses and it was the only section of the Federal defenses that had not been strongly attacked by our army in the battle.

While standing on the ridge, I was joined by Private Samuel F. Pawlett of the Eighteenth Virginia Infantry of my brigade. Samuel looked at Cemetery Ridge just as I was doing. He said, "His heart almost failed him. This is going to be a heller! Prepare for the worst!" A chaplain also approached and joined us. He observed Cemetery Ridge. His expression was filled with despair as he shook his head. He said, "It would require a very bloody battle to win the day." Others of my comrades from the brigade soon arrived, but remained silent. Their expressions revealed the thoughts and revelations of their hearts.

Officers were standing nearby and talking about the fight before us. All of us felt the gravity of the situation and realized the most astonishing work was before us. Every man felt that it was his duty to make the fight; that he was his own commander. They would have made the charge without an officer of any description. They only needed to be told what they were expected to do. All appreciated the danger and felt this would be their last charge. All were willing to die to achieve victory and end the war. The struggle at the stone fence would be intense. It would be a field of sacrifice, a field of glory, a valley of death.

It was about this time I noticed Major Dearing looking at his timepiece. General Lee and his adjutant, Colonel W. H. Taylor, rode up and dismounted. General Lee was wearing a well-worn long gray jacket, a high black felt hat, and blue trousers tucked into his Wellington boots. He did not carry any side arms. His only mark of military rank was the three stars on his collar. He was very neat in his dress. Over the last fourteen months while commanding the army, he was always neat in his dress during the most difficult marches.

After dismounting, General Lee used a tree stump to spread out a map near the position of the Fifty-Sixth Virginia Infantry. I noticed Generals Longstreet and Pickett rode up and joined them. In a few minutes, other officers arrived. It had the appearance of a council of war. Staff officers kept coming and going as the general officers looked over the map and spoke. Afterward, General Lee and the rest of the officers rode off in different directions.

A short time later, Captain Bissell explained the assault to our company. It would include three divisions, about twelve to fifteen thousand men. The divisions would include General Johnston Pettigrew and General Isaac Tremble's from General A. P. Hill's Third Corps, and our division under General Pickett. There would be a heavy bombardment by the artillery under the command of Lieutenant-Colonel Porter Alexander. When the time was right and our batteries had executed as much damage as possible by the bombardment, the infantry would form up and advance toward Cemetery Ridge. Now everyone knew what had taken place between General Lee and the other officers.

\*\*\*\*

About 1:00 o'clock in the afternoon, according to my timepiece, General Pickett rode by the guns. The artillerymen in our front raced to their guns, opened their caisson chest and pulled off their jackets. The drivers hid in the holes they had previously dug. Our officers commanded us to lie down. Suddenly there was the boom of a Napoleon gun and then another by the Washington Artillery from New Orleans near the Emmitsburg Road. It was the signal the bombardment from our artillery should commence.

Then along our lines, every artillery gun began to fire. The roar was intense. The sound of not a single gun could be distinguished.

The Federal artillery's response was immediate and vigorous to our first barrage. No sooner had the smoke cleared from our guns than Federal artillery shells began to fall among our regiment. The ground shook after the first barrage as if we were in the throes of an earthquake. The shells were howling, shrieking, and exploding. Grass and dirt sprayed the air as the ground was torn up. I recall how trees and fencing were splintered, sending fragments through the ranks to pierce flesh. Rocks and stones were sent flying when the ground was constantly hit by iron shot. I buried my head into the earth and gritted my teeth.

A shell exploded in front of me, throwing dirt over my back and neck. When I looked up, it was no more than three feet from me where the shell had exploded. I glanced around and noticed a horrified expression on a soldier's face to my right. He was dead.

As I was lying on the ground, I heard another shell explode nearby. I felt warm drops on the side of my face. I raised up and looked several feet in another direction. An artillery shell had ploughed through the bodies of two of my comrades, privates Ben Jackson and Albert Morris, cutting their bodies in two. Their blood was the warm feeling I had experienced against my face. Blood was splattered all over my clothing. Privates Jackson and Morris were friends and messmates, serving together on other fields of battle. I guess it was only appropriate that they should die together. Another soldier crawled over to help remove their remains when a shell struck the blanket he had recently occupied.

Nearly every minute the cry of mortal agony was heard above the roar and rumble of cannon. In our midst and through our ranks poured solid shot and bursting shells dealing out death on every hand. A single shell went bounding madly across the field through a line of prostrated men and rushed on with a wail to the rear leaving a wide track of blood behind. Yet the men remained at their post.

I looked off to my right and noticed some of General Kemper's men were exposed in a field and did not have as much shelter as we did. I thought the Third and Seventh Virginia Infantry regiments must be taking a pounding from the Federal artillery. Some men had been mangled beyond recognition, disintegrated by artillery explosion, and torn apart.

Men's nerves in General Garnett's brigade were being tested. Tree limbs came tumbling on some of us. The thudding sound of shell fragments constantly hitting tree trunks sounded like hail. It caused us to feel quite helpless and nervous. A few soldiers fled, but returned later. But still there was bravery among the ranks. Major Dearing rode among his artillery guns waving a flag and encouraging his artillerist to continue the fight. General Garnett did likewise among our brigade. Five men from the Eighth Virginia became casualties from the Federal bombardment.

General Armistead's brigade was behind our brigade. I don't know how they did under the bombardment. I did notice General Armistead pacing back and forward among his men. I was sure he was encouraging them. He was a Regular Army soldier before the War of Northern Aggression and was a steady man of steel nerves.

Not everyone stayed in their place. Some of the men of the Eighth became restless and were willing to defy danger. Richard Mattocks of Company C, the Blue Mountain Boys from Loudoun County, was one of those individuals. He took several canteens to a nearby house behind the ridge to fill them with water. I noticed him about fifteen minutes later returning to his company. Strange enough, Richard had discarded his cap for a straw hat that he must have taken from the house.

Not knowing what was in store for us, men began to prepare for the hereafter in many ways. I noticed Major Berkeley of our regiment removing his pack of playing cards from his possession and placing them in a hole under a rock. It was considered a sin by some of the religions for a man to indulge in such sport. Another man was praying and reciting the Lord's Prayer. Even in the midst all of the confusion and battle, I briefly opened my Testament and glanced at the Gospel of John where I read "God so loved the world that he gave his only begotten Son that whosoever believed in him should have everlasting life." Even though I believed, it was still a comfort and reassurance to my personal faith.

I thought of Sarah and the boys. I did not know by the end of this fight if I would find favor with God and be given the chance to see them another day. Like everyone else in this army, I hoped it would be the end and that all of us, both blue and gray could return home to be with our families. I only wished I could have sent Sarah a few lines in a correspondence and told her I loved her and the boys.

I looked up again and noticed a deep white haze had filled the air. The whole valley was enveloped in it. The haze made it difficult to see. The sun lately so glaring, was by that time obscured. Nothing could be seen but the flashing light leaping from the cannon's mouths amidst the surrounding smoke. The smell of acrid smoke burned my nose. The cannonade was terrific. It was far worse than anything I had witnessed or experienced thus far in this war. The gunners splendidly worked their guns in the face of danger and won the admiration of the infantry.

From what I could notice, the artillery was taking a pounding from their Federal adversaries. The Federal artillerists had demonstrated their skill. I noticed caissons had been damaged, and some guns were disabled because of damaged gun carriages. There were casualties among the horses and men.

At one point during the heavy cannonade, I watched with admiration as General Lee and one staff officer passed between the artillery guns and our men. I could not help but to admire General

Lee for his courage, allowing himself needlessly to be placed in immediate danger. It both horrified and thrilled me. When many of the men yelled to General Lee to go away and seek shelter, he removed his hat in acknowledgement of their affection and then rode at a faster pace on his gray horse.

We all knew now it would be just a matter of time before the command came for us to form into battle formation and begin the advance across the field. Tensions were high. The spirits of the men were willing.

*Source: Library of Congress*

**Major-General Robert Milroy**

*Source: National Archives*

**Major-General Winfield Scott Hancock**

Source: National Archives

**Major-General George Meade**

*Source: Authors Collection*

**Brigadier-General Robert B. Garnett**

*Source: Author's Collection*

**Major-General George Pickett**

*Source: Author's Collection*

**Colonel Eppa Hunton**

*Source: National Archives*

**Lieutenant-General James Longstreet**

*Source: National Archives*

**General Robert E. Lee**

## Chapter Seventeen

It was about 3:00 o'clock according to my timepiece, when General Longstreet or "Old Pete" as he was called, rode out in front of the men along the ridge from right to left. He possessed a magnificent grace and composure. His bearing was to me the grandest morale spectacle of the war. I expected to see him fall. Still, he moved on slowly and majestically with an inspiring confidence, composure, self-possession, and repressed power in every movement and look that fascinated me.

I remember General Longstreet being over six feet tall, weighing about two hundred pounds. He was physically striking and was often smoking a cigar. General Longstreet was known as a fighter and probably the best Corps commander in the army. He was known in the First Corps as General Lee's "Old War Horse." Most of the time, he was seen with General Lee.

General Longstreet wanted to inspire and encourage the men so they did not become faint-hearted. Shells continued to fall everywhere but not with the same intensity as earlier. General Longstreet was escorted by one staff officer, Lieutenant-Colonel Moxley Sorrel. General Longstreet was in plain view of the Federals. It was General Longstreet's intentions to inspect our lines before the grand assault.

A few Yankee artillery shells ploughed up the ground around General Longstreet. He had to calm his horse, but without fear or hesitation, he continued to ride along the line. We believed General Longstreet was going to lead the assault against Cemetery Ridge. The men called out, "get to the rear" and "we'll fight without you leading us." After the men's admonishment, General Longstreet rode leisurely and calmly into the woods. General

Longstreet's men had a great amount of respect for him because from their testimonies, he led by example, always being in the thick of things.

When General Longstreet disappeared into the wooded area, General Pickett shortly emerged from the same area. He dashed along the line calling the whole division to attention. Every soldier jumped to his feet, cheering and even giving the Rebel Yell. When I jumped up to answer the call, I must have scared a rabbit because the creature frantically zigzagged to the rear. I cannot say that I blamed him. We were ordered by company lots to pile our blankets and extra gear because we were told we would not be needing them where we were going.

Afterward, I fixed my bayonet on my Springfield rifle. The time had come for the grand assault against the Federal position along Cemetery Ridge. I noticed there were a number of men who did not get up from what appeared to be sunstroke. One soldier in particular not far from me was experiencing dreadful contortions of the body with foaming at the mouth, and was almost lifeless. In this business there are those that are gallantly dead, who will never charge again; the helplessly wounded; the men who have charged on many a battlefield, but are now helpless from the heat and sun; and the men in whom there is not sufficient courage to enable them to rise. These last were few.

My regiment, the Eighth Virginia, was on the right with the Eighteenth, Nineteenth, Twenty-Eighth, and Fifty-Sixth Virginia to our left in battle line formation. General Kemper's brigade was to our brigade's right and General Armistead's was behind our brigade as a support. The regiments of my brigade took some time to dress ranks. We dressed on the left. Our company, like every other company, was formed in double rank battle line formation. Equal number of men from my company made up the front-rank line with the company's captain on the right and there were equal numbers of men that made up the rear rank. I was beside Captain Bissell on the front rank or line. Behind the second rank line were three sergeants and two lieutenants as file closers. General Pickett's division stretched for about half-a-mile.

Each regiment in the brigade contributed a company of men to fight as skirmishers. Skirmishers were men that were lightly armed and used for increased battlefield movement. They were usually armed with a weapon of good range to attack the enemy at a distance. They would move in front of the brigade, challenging the Federal skirmishers. Once we were close enough to the Emmitsburg Road, they would be the first to attempt to pull down the stake-and-rider fence. Company H was chosen to be skirmishers to fulfill this duty for the Eighth Virginia. This was the same company that my new acquaintance and friend Randolph Shotwell belonged to. I said a short prayer for him.

It was still exceedingly hot. There was a slight breeze, causing the Virginia flags to flutter, but it was not cool enough to give us much relief from the heat. The men were tense. The strain of the work before us was evident on each expression. Everyone was expecting to move forward any minute. I overheard a soldier anxiously say that he "never expected to get out alive" The soldier continued, "No better men went into battle than our division" and "more dangerous place was hard to find to put them in." I continued to think of my family. Would I survive this ordeal and be reunited with them once more?

I watched as General Garnett sat on his bay horse, Red Eye. He spoke with the regimental officers of our brigade. Other than Colonel Hunton, he was one of the few officers that took part in the charge on horseback. All the other officers were on foot. I can still vividly recall General Garnett dressed in his finest uniform coat, buttoned to the top. He wore an almost new pair of trousers and spurs on his boots. General Garnett turned and rode to the front of the brigade in a soldierly fashion. As he did so, one of the captains led us in a hymn and then a white-haired chaplain stepped forward. He knelt and somberly prayed. It had come to this; prayers and valor. It was every man's chance to make peace with God before the killing, maiming, and destruction of battle began.

After everyone finished praying, General Pickett rode up in front of the Eighteenth Virginia. He appeared graceful with his cap well over his right ear and long auburn locks nicely dressed, hanging almost to his shoulders. General Pickett pointed toward Cemetery Ridge and shouted, "Boys, you see that battery? I want you to take those guns. Remember you are Virginians." Afterward, Generals Pickett and Garnett were close to where I was standing in line. I overheard General Pickett say to General Garnett, "Get across the field as soon as you can because I believe you are going to catch hell. It is a devilish ugly place over yonder and we can't afford to let them double teams on us."

With General Pickett's exhortations, it was time. General Garnett shouted he "would lead his division and that death was near to all." Captain Bissell informed us to advance slowly, arms at will. There was to be no cheering, no firing, no breaking from common to quick step. Dress on the center. As the brigade moved forward, drummer boys began to beat the cadence, musicians played patriotic airs and General Garnett waved his hat, cheering the men on.

As we neared the Spangler farm buildings, Lieutenant-Colonel E. P. Alexander of the artillery rode over and spoke briefly with General Garnett and then parted. Our artillerymen from Major Dearing's battalion along the ridge lifted their red kepi caps in a salute. They knew they had done all they could do and now it was up to the foot soldier to carry the dreadful ridge before us. One artillerymen cried out "Give it to 'em boys; we've got 'em demoralized; and you'uns can make 'em git up and dust out'm dirt piles!"

General Pickett and four aides, Captains Baird, Symington, Bright, and Major Charles Pickett, the General's brother, fell in about twenty yards in the rear of the column. This was a good place for General Pickett to keep abreast of things and to issue orders. General Pickett, I believe, felt a sense of pride that Virginians were called on to possibly decide this affair.

As we marched forward, it appeared as if we were on dressed parade, always dressing our ranks and keeping the proper formation. Our battle flags and regimental flags were snapping in the breeze. The glistening sunlight shined brightly on bayonets and officers' swords. I can still recall the long lines of men moving across the farmland at a steady pace. All of us were dressed in gray or butternut-colored coats, and some wore slouched hats, kepis or high beehive hats. All of us were dirty and sweaty, but we always kept our muskets in perfect working order. Many of the soldiers were much younger than me. We appeared as ragged scarecrows. Our clothing was patched and well-worn. Our feet were clad in roughshod brogans. Quite a few were barefooted. No matter what our appearance, we were all determined to see the struggle through to the end.

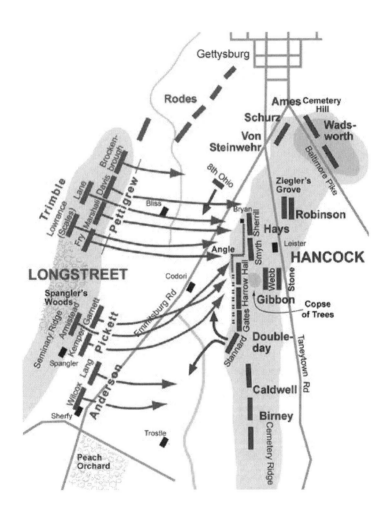

Pickett's Charge, July 3, 1863

110

## *Chapter Eighteen*

General Garnett shouted, "Steady, men! Close up! A little faster; not too fast! Save your strength!" We were still far away from Cemetery Ridge where we were unable to pick up the pace. There was grim silence among the ranks. All three brigades managed to keep a good alignment even though we had to cross a fence not too far from the artillery line. Company C of the Twenty-Eighth Virginia managed to move ahead of the front line of the brigade, but were shortly corrected and fell back into line.

At first when the Federal artillery spotted us, they did not react. I do not know why unless they were amazed at our gallantry. We were a splendid target. No sooner than I had given thought to this, suddenly off in the distance, I could see the white puffs of smoke from their Dogs of War. They began to throw everything in their arsenal at us. Shot, shell, spherical case, whatever artillery shells they possessed, they used. As we continued across the field, I noticed the air was filled with deadly missiles, all coming in our direction. Some exploded in the air while others exploded on the ground throwing dirt upon us and causing fire to erupt in the field where we were marching.

Whenever a shell exploded near the brigade's battle line, it caused destruction. I witnessed many times the explosion of a single Yankee artillery percussion shell. Percussion shells were intended to explode on contact cutting out several files of men. One of these shells exploded in our brigade ranks, causing terrible devastation. One company from the Fifty-Sixth Virginia was almost swept to a man because of one of these shells. The officers ordered the survivors to close their ranks while still others stepped over the dead. Five or six wounded turned back and gave up the fight. I heard a soldier in the second rank or battle line say "truly does the work of death begin." Some men that were slightly wounded, as well as those who would not harden themselves when the struggle began to get desperate, headed back toward Seminary Ridge.

In the Nineteenth Virginia, a shell exploded, causing quite a few men to go down to the ground. I heard the shout of an officer "now boys, put your trust in God and follow me." It had some effect on those soldiers nearby because they responded to the officer's plea. The lines closed and serenely moved on as unfaltering as before. Every movement expressed determination and resolute defiance. The line moved forward like a victorious giant, confident of power and victory. What was the inspiration, I thought that gave them the stout courage, the gallantry, the fearlessness, the steadiness, the collective and individual heroism? It was home, patriotism, and the high sense of duty. It was the call to honor.

Throughout the brigade, officers continued to order us to close up the line because of the gaps caused by the Federal artillery. To this point, we were still well out of Federal infantry musket range. Only a few were killed and injured in my regiment. It was not enough to affect our march.

Off in the distance, I noticed our skirmishers were engaged with the Yankee skirmishers. It looked as though our boys had dismantled some fencing and had stacked it for use as protection against the Yankees. Our skirmishers continued to stay there until we approached and then they rejoined the main battle line.

General Kemper's brigade as well as our brigade were in full view of Cemetery Ridge and the Round Tops. We needed to begin the maneuver which was necessary to unite the left of our division and the right of General Pettigrew's division into one battle line for the final surge toward the Federals along Cemetery Ridge. This order was known as a left oblique. A left oblique means that each soldier in the whole division had to turn forty-five degrees to the left so that the whole line sidled toward General Pettigrew's division without compromising our alignment. There was some confusion in the ranks, but we managed to accomplish the maneuver. We could not see the main Federal infantry battle line along the stone fence on Cemetery Ridge, but our right flank was exposed to their artillery. The Federal artillery was in a position where they could fire on the whole length of our march and battle line formation.

As we approached the fence line bordering the Emmitsburg Road, Federal artillery became most troublesome and was beginning to take its toll on the brigade. The Yankees opened a withering fire of musketry near the Emmitsburg Road. We paused and fired a volley. Many of the Yankees took off running. Some of us believed we had defeated the first line, but we would shortly discover that was not so. The Federals we engaged were only a heavy skirmish line. One of the bullets from the brief fight struck Colonel Hunton in the leg while he was riding behind our regiment. His horse was also hit by the same bullet as it passed through the Colonel's leg. Colonel Hunton and his horse returned to Seminary Ridge for aid.

Command of the regiment fell to one of the Berkeley brothers. Lieutenant- Colonel Norborne Berkeley was next to the youngest of the four brothers and was considered a brave individual. I recalled hearing Colonel Hunton speak of the brothers when I first joined up with the Eighth Virginia at Berryville. Colonel Hunton said to another officer at his headquarters' tent. "They were four of the bravest, noblest, most patriotic and unselfish men. They were always ready for any duty they were called upon to perform, and always did it with alacrity, courage and efficiency."

Under Lieutenant-Colonel Berkeley's leadership, we came to the Emmitsburg Road and the stake-and-rider fence. The fence line bordered each side of the road and was at least five feet high. This stopped all forward movement of the brigade. We tried to tear down the fence. Some soldiers were striking it with the butt of their muskets. We had no other choice than to climb over each fence since it was too sturdy for us to tear down. Before climbing, I witnessed some of the worst destruction done to the brigade thus far in the assault. Since the fence was so high, the men made good targets. Men were falling all around and cannon and volleys of musketry were raining death upon many. Men were falling backward into the field and forward into the sunken road.

I was breathing heavily. The sweat was running off of my forehead. I said a little prayer not knowing if I would make it any further. I could hear the distinct sound of bullets and shell fragments striking the stake-and-rider fence like pelting rain. Without further hesitation, I climbed over the fence while listening to the whizzing sound of missiles flying past my body. When I jumped down, I fell on a comrade who was lying face down. He did not moan. I knew he was dead.

I noticed hundreds of men were lying in the sunken road and refusing to climb the second fencerow. Officers tried to rally the men, even striking some with the blunt end of their swords, but to no avail. It had been too desperate and too much of a slaughter climbing the first fencerow for the men to try the second row and maybe die in the attempt. I turned and looked down the Emmitsburg Road where General Pettigrew's men were also crossing the fence. I was terrified by all that I was witnessing. Men were dropping from the fence as if swept by a gigantic sickle swung by some powerful force of nature. Great gaps were formed in the line. The numbers of slain and wounded could not be estimated by numbers, but must be measured by yards.

I believed it was my duty to continue. I said another prayer and climbed the second fence. When I jumped to my feet after scaling the fence, those soldiers with great determination and vengeance followed.

Once over the fence, many of our men were mingled with the Third Virginia of General Kemper's brigade in an orchard. There was hardly any organization among any of the regiments of the brigade. All was confusion. Musketry fire began coming in against the flank of our attacking column. Some of the men from my regiment deliberately turned and began battling the new enemy, who were about seventy yards away while others shot forward toward the crest of Cemetery Ridge to renew the attack on the stone fence in the distance.

One wing of my regiment passed to the south of the farmhouse along the Emmitsburg Road while the other passed to the north. My company passed to the north and for a moment was sheltered from the Federal fire. Major Edmund Berkeley and shortly thereafter his brother William, the captain of Company D, were wounded.

I looked up the slope of Cemetery Ridge and saw a dense blue line rising from beyond the earthworks on the crest. Sheets of withering and blinding blaze like a volcano burst forth from the muzzles of many muskets. While urging the men forward, Lieutenant-Colonel Norborne Berkeley fell wounded.

Shells and bullets continued to come in on our front and flank. The dull thud of Minnie balls hitting the men, and their screams from being hit made one continuous noise amid the fury of war. The bearer of our regimental standard was shot down. Another picked up the flag and he was also shot down.

On and up the slope of Cemetery Ridge we steadily swept without a sound or shot, save as men would clamor to be allowed to return fire that was being poured into them. About one hundred yards away, we were allowed by General Garnett to fire and holler. The yell was so loud and strong that it was inspiring. The earth trembled.

As we got closer to the stone fence, there was no regimental or brigade organization among General Garnett's men. Every regiment was mingled with each other and in great disorder. By now, most of the bearers of the regimental colors had been shot down. We were so close to the Federals that I could see the expressions on their faces. Not far from the stone fence, I noticed the Federals were hastily deserting their cannons. Their infantry began to follow and race with terror toward a copse of trees behind the cannons. There, many began to reform their ranks to carry on the struggle. Still, there were those Federals who refused to reform their ranks, but instead raced over the crest of Cemetery Ridge.

We were about twenty-five feet away. General Garnett was waving his black hat, commanding, "Faster men, faster! We are almost there!" Many of the men knew what was coming because they pulled their caps down over their eyes and bowed their heads forward while advancing as do men when walking against a hailstorm. There was a volley of musketry by the Federals not far from the stone fence. Many of the men that had bowed their heads foward went down while the survivors recoiled under the volley. General Garnett was shot dead from his horse. I knew with him so exposed on his horse it would only be a matter of time. By now most of the officers in the brigade were casualties.

I was near the front and was sure the next volley would get me. I fell to the ground to save my life the best that I could. To go back under such a hailstorm of lead and bullets was risky and insane. I began crawling under the cover of the white haze that had just been created by the volleys of musketry. Another Confederate volley was fired bringing down a large number of the same group of Federals who had just fired on us not far from the stone fence. I stayed on the ground, believing the Federals would soon reply again with another withering volley of musketry. Beside of me laid one of the Farr boys from my Company. He was a pious youth. He lay with his hands clasped, singing a hymn, waiting on death to arrive. I had never experienced war so deadly. We were in a whirlpool of hell and there seemed to be no way out.

*Source: Sue Boardman*

**Emmitsburg Road**

## *Chapter Nineteen*

General Armistead and his brigade were several hundred yards behind us when we began the attack from Seminary Ridge. By now, General Armistead and what was left of his brigade had arrived near the stone fence where I was located. Lieutenant-Colonel Rawley Martin of the Fifty-Third Virginia Infantry was near General Armistead. Over the noise of battle, I heard General Armistead shout "Martin? We can't stay here, we must go over the wall."

Lieutenant-Colonel Martin agreed and instantly jumped over the stone fence, which was very low in this area. He commanded, "forward with the colors." No sooner than the words departed from his mouth, he was shot down with a wound in the thigh.

After witnessing Lieutenant-Colonel Martin shot down, General Armistead held aloft his hat-tipped sword and cried, "Come on, boys, give them the cold steel." With this command, General Armistead was able to inspire a few hundred faithful men to follow him over the wall. As he continued to inspire and lead his men, I was not one of them.

General Armistead was leading his men from the front, as do faithful and true leaders. He charged with his men for another twenty to thirty yards. While still waving his hat-tipped sword aloft, he placed his hand on one of the cannons and was shot down by the Federals. General Armistead fell under the abandoned Yankee artillery guns, his hat and sword almost striking one of the cannons. General Armistead still grasped his sword. At the time, I thought he was dead, but learned later after the war that he lived until the next day.

Our little band of men did not stand a chance because more and more Federal soldiers were arriving. It would only be a matter of time before our men were all killed if we did not surrender. Our men courageously continued the struggle, believing that fresh brigades and divisions of our men from Seminary Ridge would support us. I glanced more than once back over the field we had crossed. I did not see any reinforcements coming to our support. I was grieved and disappointed because if we had been supported by fresh troops, we stood a chance of winning the battle and maybe the beginning of gaining our independence and returning home with our families.

I continued to reload and fire my musket as fast as I could from behind the stone fence at the converging Federal infantrymen. They formed a line on three sides around General Armistead's men. At one point, I believed I was loading and firing three rounds a minute. Because I was firing so fast, the weapon became so hot I had to pause for a moment to allow the barrel to cool down so I could continue to use the weapon.

Not far from me along the stone fence, I recognized six of my comrades from the Eighth Virginia. They were Lieutenants Charles Berkeley and Ben Hutchison of Company D, together with Sergeant A. H. Compton, John Swartz, and the two Lunceford brothers of Company C. I quickly glanced down the line at Corporal Ben Lunceford, who was also firing over the stone fence while his brother Evans loaded for him. We appeared to be the only remnants left of the Eighth Virginia. I believed at the time my regiment had been totally destroyed.

I laid the hot weapon to the side. While lying on the ground, I watched the struggle taking place on the other side of the stone fence. Somewhere in my heart, I believed this to be our last great attempt at breaking through the Federal line of defense.

On the inside of what would be known later as the angle of the stonewall fence, our men were in plain view of the Federal officers. They could see that my comrades were exhausted by what we had already accomplished. Even over the sound of battle, and being too far away to hear commands, I could tell by the Federal officers' gestures with waving swords aloft, they were exhorting and rallying their men to stand their ground and continue the struggle to the finish.

On both sides there were oaths declared, curses toward one

another, hurrahs of small victories, and shouts of defiance and exhortations. Our men and the Federals came so close to each other that they fired their weapons not more than five feet apart. Flames scorched their clothing, causing their uniform coats to catch fire. Some soldiers threw down their muskets and fought fist to fist while others used their muskets as clubs. Human life was cheap, and the wrath and fury of war was being satisfied with the shedding of blood.

I witnessed a private from the Fifty-Sixth Virginia whirl around and catch a Yankee in the stomach with his cold steel. I was sure my comrade had killed him instantly. There were bayonet thrusts by both sides, saber strokes, the crackle of pistol shots, and cool deliberate movements on the part of both sides. Men were going down on their hands and knees, spinning around like tops, throwing out their arms, and coughing up blood. On that day I witnessed a recklessness of life, tenacity of purpose, and a fiery determination, unequal to anything I had ever witnessed and experienced. It was such that the War of Northern Aggression I thought would be decided on that fateful day, at that fateful moment.

The struggle must have continued for about twenty minutes. I could not watch the outpouring of blood and lives continue any longer. There was not an officer above the rank of captain among our men to give an order to retreat or continue the struggle. I knew it was only a matter of time and the fighting would end. I turned and walked away, leaving my weapon lying on the ground near the stone fence.

I continued to turn around and look from time to time as I walked toward the fence bordering the Emmitsburg Road. The fighting was still continuing. Occasionally a bullet would make a hissing sound as it passed by my body. If shot by a Federal soldier, I hoped it would be while I was facing the stone fence rather then have my back turned toward it. I did not desire that Sarah and the boys would think of me as some kind of a coward. I was fortunate I was not shot from behind. I found out later that General Wilcox's division had attacked as ordered but withdrew after a few volleys, seeing the uselessness of the assault against Cemetery Ridge. I guess it was because of his assault that the Federals were preoccupied, allowing some of my comrades and me to get away without being shot or captured.

What I witnessed on my way back to Seminary Ridge was as mortifying as all that I observed at the stone fence. I never saw dead and wounded men lay so thick. From a space about seventy-feet back to the opposite side of the pike I could have walked over the dead bodies of men. The canister fire from the Federal Dogs of War had devastated the bodies of our men. Heads were shot off, limbs were shot off, men were shot in two, men were shot into pieces, and little fragments here and there were hardly recognizable to me. Still, the shrieks and groans of the dying filled the air. Their many cries were pitiful. Some prayed while others expressed the most fearful oaths. No one knows or has any idea of what it was like, the pain, the misery of those poor fellows who had been shot down. I could not comfort them. It was just like a graveyard.

Along the Emmitsburg Road, it was a perfect slaughter. I knelt beside a wounded soldier. My knees were soaked in human blood. I gave him a drink of water. He was silent, his eyes gazing somberly on me. Tears filled my eyes as I lay him back on the ground to die and moved to another. I took my canteen, which by now was almost empty and began to give a drink of water to others of my wounded and brave comrades in arms. My canteen was empty. I filled it from a ditch along the road; not giving any thought the water was mingled with the blood of the dead and dying. I did not know what else to do.

Source: Sue Boardman

**Copse of Trees at Cemetery Ridge**

## *Chapter Twenty*

As I continued across the open field back to Seminary Ridge, the Federal artillery fire increased. West of our artillery batteries, I turned and noticed many more of my comrades returning to the safety of Seminary Ridge. As I watched, the men were in small broken parties, others walked supported by two muskets as crutches, still others received assistance from comrades who were not as hurt as themselves, and others were carried on stretchers by the ambulance corps. It was an unbelievable sight. The Army of Northern Virginia had been badly defeated. When I turned around, shells continued to explode among the trees, causing their limbs to fall to the ground nearby.

I met up with Randolph Shotwell. Both of us were so exhausted we could hardly walk. General Lee arrived. We immediately saluted the commanding general. General Lee asked, "Are you wounded?"

"No, general, only a little fatigued; but I am afraid there are but few so lucky as myself," Private Shotwell replied.

"Ah! Yes, I am very sorry," General Lee answered in a sad voice, "The task was too great for you. But we mustn't despond. Another time we shall succeed. Are you one of Pickett's men?"

"Yes, sir."

"Well, you had better go back and rest yourself. Captain Linthicum will tell you the rendezvous for your brigade," General Lee said.

Captain Charles Linthicum was the former chaplain of my regiment. Now he was serving as Adjutant General of General Garnett's brigade.

As we were saluting General Lee, another soldier passed by waving a flag and saying, "General, let us go it again!"

My friend Private Shotwell departed, but I was still too

exhausted to continue. I stood in the same spot for a moment, still resting. General Pickett rode up to General Lee. General Lee said, "General Pickett, place your division in the rear of this hill, and be ready to repel the advance of the enemy should they follow up their advantage."

I could see the tears streaming down General Pickett's cheeks. He bowed his head and replied in a broken voice, "General Lee, I have no division now. Armistead is down, Garnett is down, and Kemper is mortally wounded."

"Come, General Pickett, this has been my fight, and upon my shoulders rests the blame. The men and officers of your command have written the name of Virginia as high today as it has ever been written."

With General Lee's statement, I walked away and went looking for Captain Linthicum. I noticed later during the afternoon that General Pickett was not the only general in tears. Generals Hill and Wilcox were reported to have been crying too.

As for the men among the ranks, some were throwing away their blankets, gear, and weapons. I watched all this and believed the army was coming apart. But that did not happen. General Lee's army would, upon their arrival back in Virginia, regain their strength and courage. We would continue the struggle for our independence for almost two more years and fight the Army of the Potomac again on another battlefield.

Later that evening when my regiment had roll call, there were only thirty-four of us from the Eighth Virginia Infantry out of two hundred twelve from this morning who answered the call to duty. We had suffered as I would later be informed by Private Shotwell, thirty-nine killed, seventy-nine wounded, and sixty captured. We had truly earned the nickname "The Bloody Eighth" after Gettysburg. Many of our field officers were killed, wounded or captured.

At the time I did not know these facts that I now commit to paper, but I found out years later at a Confederate reunion in Richmond, Virginia. In General Garnett's brigade we lost nine hundred and forty-one men out of over one thousand, three hundred engaged. The casualties for the whole division under General Pickett were terrifying. General Pickett's division lost three thousand four hundred men out of five thousand engaged that fateful Friday. I remembered at that same reunion the next morning after the charge on Cemetery Ridge, the division could only muster about one thousand six hundred men fit for duty.

Many of the men from the Eighth Virginia Infantry, who I marched into Pennsylvania with, were not as fortunate as me. The few who actually reached the stone fence were captured. The only other person to escape captivity other then myself was Evans Luceford. As for Captain Bissell's fate, I later learned that he had been wounded and had died. Captain Bissell and I had become separated during the fighting between the Emmitsburg Road and Cemetery Ridge. Private Alfred Rollins, another comrade, who I had met at Berryville, and shared some meaningful evenings in conversation around the campfire with, was also killed somewhere on Cemetery Ridge.

Friday, July 3, 1863, was a sorrowful day for Virginia. Some of its best flesh and blood had served with gallantry and distinction that day. It was a hard thing to leave the wounded behind, but the army was in no condition to carry on the campaign. Men were too broken up and demoralized by the struggle on that day. We had been completely cut up. All of us came to Pennsylvania with high hopes and expectations that one more major victory would end the war. We could all go home to our families and firesides. Now there were many of my comrades from Virginia who would never return home.

On that day, I thought of Sarah and the boys. The Northern newspapers were sure to publish their glorious victory at Gettysburg. Sarah would worry, I knew.

In the coming days, when able, I sent Sarah a correspondence and informed her of my welfare. I was fortunate I had received God's grace. On that day along Seminary Ridge, I thought, poor Virginia bled again at every pore. There would be few firesides in her midst where the voice of mourning would not be heard when the black-lettered list of losses was published. In concluding my recollections on this hallowed field, I believed then as well as now that General Pickett's division gained nothing but glory from this battle. As for my brave comrades of General Pickett's division, they will be forever immortalized at **Gettysburg: The Field of Glory.**

*Source: Courtesy of the Library of Congress*

**General Pickett's men at the Bloody Angle**

## Major Charles S. Peyton's Report

Major Charles S. Peyton of the Nineteenth Virginia Infantry was the only officer from Brigadier-General Robert Garnett's brigade that was not killed or wounded in the assault on Cemetery Ridge by General Pickett's division. Major Peyton temporarily commanded the remnants of General Garnett's brigade after the battle. Major Peyton wrote the following report:

*Camp near Williamsport, MD. July 9, 1863*

*Major: In compliance with instructions from division headquarters, I have the honor to report the part taken by this brigade in the late battle near Gettysburg, Pa July 3.*

*Notwithstanding the long and severe marches made by the troops of this brigade, they reached the field about 9 a. m. in high spirits and in good condition. At 12 we were ordered to take a position behind the crest of the hill on which the artillery, under Colonel E. Porter Alexander, was planted, where we lay during a most terrific cannonading, which opened at 1:30 p. m., and was kept up without intermission for one hour.*

*During the shelling, we lost about 20 killed and wounded. Among the killed was Lieutenant-Colonel John T. Ellis, of the Nineteenth Virginia, whose bravery as a soldier, and his innocence, purity, and integrity as a Christian, have not only elicited the admiration of his own command, but endeared him to all who knew him.*

*At 2:30 p. m., the artillery fire having to some extent abated, the order to advance was given, first by Major-General Pickett in person, and repeated by General Garnett with promptness,* apparent cheerfulness, and alacrity. The brigade moved forward at quick time. The ground was open, but little broken, and from 800 to 1,000 yards from the crest whence we started to the enemy's line. The brigade moved in good order, keeping up its line almost perfectly, notwithstanding it had to climb three high post and rail fences, behind the last of which the enemy's skirmishers were first met and immediately driven in. Moving on, we soon met the advance line of the enemy, lying concealed in the grass on the slope, about 100 yards in front of his second line, which consisted of a stone wall about breast-high running nearly parallel to and about 30 paces from the crest of the hill, which was lined with their artillery.

The first line referred to above after offering some resistance, was completely routed, and driven in confusion back to the stone wall. Here we captured some prisoners, which were ordered to the rear without a guard. Having routed the enemy here, General Garnett ordered the brigade forward, which it promptly obeyed, loading and firing as it advanced.

Up to this time we had suffered but little from the enemy's batteries, which apparently had been much crippled previous to our advance, with the exception of one posted on the mountain, about 1 mile to our right, which enfiladed nearly our entire line with fearful effect, some times as many as 10 men being killed and wounded by the bursting of a single shell. From the point it had first routed the enemy, the brigade moved rapidly forward toward the stone wall, under a galling fire both from artillery and infantry, the artillery using grape and canister. We were now within 75 paces of the wall, unsupported on the right and left, General Kemper being some 50 or 60 yards behind and to the right, and General Armistead coming up in our rear.

General Kemper's line was discovered to be lapping on ours, when deeming it advisable to have the line extended on the right to prevent being flanked, a staff officer rode back to the general to request him to incline to the right. General Kemper not being present (perhaps wounded at the time), Captain W. T. Fry, of his staff, immediately began his exertions to carry out the request, but, in consequence of the eagerness of the men pressing forward, it was impossible to have the order carried out.

Our line much shattered, still kept up the advance until within about 20 paces of the wall, when, for a moment, it recoiled under the terrific fire that poured into our ranks both from their batteries and their sheltered infantry. At this moment, General Kemper came up on the right and General Armistead in rear, when the three lines, joining in concert, rushed forward with unyielding determination and an apparent spirit of laudable rivalry to plant the Southern banner on the walls of the enemy. His strongest and last line was instantly gained; the Confederate battle-flag waved over his defenses, and the fighting over the wall became hand-to hand, and of the most desperate character; but more than half having already fallen, our line was found too weak to rout the enemy. We hoped for support on the left (which had started simultaneously with ourselves), our hope in vain. Yet a small remnant remained in desperate struggle, receiving a fire in front, on the right, and on the left, many even climbing over the wall, and fighting the enemy in his own trenches until entirely surrounded; and those who were not killed or wounded were captured, with the exception of about 300 who came off slowly, but greatly scattered, the identity of every regiment being entirely lost, and every regimental commander killed or wounded.

The brigade went into action with 1,287 men and about 140 officers, as shown by the report of the previous evening, and sustained a loss, as the list of casualties will show, 941 killed, wounded, and missing, and it is feared, from all the information received, that the majority (those reported missing) are either killed or wounded.

It is needless, perhaps, to speak of conspicuous gallantry where all behaved so well. Each and every regimental commander displayed a cool bravery and daring that not only encouraged their own command, but won the highest admiration from all those who saw them. They led their regiments in the fight, and showed by their conduct, that they were willing to lead. But of our cool, gallant, noble brigade commander it may not be out of place to speak. Never had the brigade been better handled, and never has it done better service in the field of battle. There was scarcely an officer or man in the command whose attention was not attracted by the cool and handsome bearing of General Garnett, who, totally devoid of excitement or rashness, rode immediately in rear of his advancing line, endeavoring by his personal efforts, and by the aid of his staff, to keep his line well closed and dressed. He was shot from his horse while near the center of the brigade, within about 25 paces of the stone wall. This gallant officer was too well known to need further mention.

Captain C. P. Linthicum, assistant adjutant-general, Lieutenant John S. Jones, aide-de-camp, and Lieutenant Harrison, acting aide-de-camp, did their whole duty, and won the admiration of the entire command by their gallant bearing on the field while carrying orders from one portion of the line to the other, where it seemed almost impossible for any one to escape.

The conduct of Captain Michael P. Spessard, of the Twenty-eighth Virginia, was particularly conspicuous. His son fell mortally wounded, at his side; he stopped but for a moment to look on his dying son, gave him his canteen of water, and pressed on, with his company, to the wall, which he climbed, and fought the enemy with his sword in their own trenches until his sword was wrested from his hands by two Yankees; he finally made his escape to safety.

In the above report, I have endeavored to be as accurate as possible, but have had to rely mainly for information on others, whose position gave then little better opportunity for witnessing the conduct of the entire brigade than I could have, being with, and paying attention to, my own regiment.

I am, major, with great respect, your obedient servant

*Chas. S. Peyton*

*Major, Commanding*

*Maj. C. Pickett*

*Asst. Adjt. Gen., Pickett's Division*

# Northern Newspaper Accounts

Northern newspapers quickly published the events surrounding the third day's fighting at Gettysburg. This article appeared in the *Philadelphia Inquirer* on July 7, 1863.

*Then there was a lull, and we knew the Rebel infantry was charging. And splendidly they did this work, the highest and severest test of the stuff that soldiers are made of. Hill's Division, in line of battle, came first on the double-quick, their muskets at the "right shoulder shift." Longstreet came as the support, at the usual distance, with war cries and a savage insolence as yet untutored by defeat. They rushed in perfect order across the open field, up to the very muzzles of the guns, which tore lanes through them as they came. But they met men who were their equals in spirit, and their superiors in tenacity. There never was better fighting since Thermopylae than was done yesterday by our infantry and artillery. The Rebels were over our defenses. They had cleared our cannoniers and horses from one of the guns, and were whirling it around to use upon us. The bayonet drove them back. But so hard press was this brave infantry that at one time, from the exhaustion of their ammunition, every battery upon the principal crest of attack was silent, except Crowen's. His service of grape and canister was awful. It in able our line, outnumbered two to one, first to beat back Longstreet, and then to charge upon him, and take a great number of prisoners. Strange sight! So terrible was our musketry and artillery fire that when Armistead's brigade was checked in its charge, and stood reeling, all of its men dropped their muskets and crawled on their hands and knees underneath the stream of shot close to our troops, where they* made signs of surrendering. They passed through our ranks scarcely noticed, and slowly went down the slope to the road in the rear.

*Harper's Weekly* released this article on July 25, 1863, twenty-two days after the fighting at Gettysburg. This section of the article covers the Pickett, Pettigrew, Tremble Charge.

*From the woods of short, scrubby timber and the rocks near the seminary there rose a yell. It was a long loud, unremitting, hideous screech from thousands of voices. At the yell the Federal cannon opened. Soon the enemy column emerged from the woods. They came as a rush down the hill, waving arms and screeching. They climbed the fences and rushed along, each one bent upon getting first into the cemetery. The cannon roared, and grape and canister and spherical case fell thick among them. Still they rushed onward, hundreds falling out of the line. They came within musket-shot of the Federal troops. Then the small-arms began to rattle. The Confederates approached the outer line of the works. They were laboring up the hill. As they mounted the low bank of the rifle-pits, the Federal soldiers retreated out of the ditch behind, turning and firing as they went along. It was a hand-to-hand conflict. Every man fought by himself and for himself. Myriads of the enemy pushed forward down the hill, across into the works, and up to the cemetery. All were shouting and screaming, and swearing clashing their arms and firing their pieces. The enemy shells flew over the field upon the Federals artillerist on the hills above. These almost disregarding the storm which raged around them, directed all their fire upon the surging columns of the enemy's charge. Every available cannon on the Cemetery Hill, and to the right and left, threw its shells and shots into the valley. The fight was terrible; but despite every effort the enemy pushed up the hill and across the second line of works. The fire became hotter. The fight swayed back and forth. Several attempts were made to take the place, but they were not successful; and late in the afternoon, leaving dead and wounded behind them, the enemy's force slowly retreated upon their own hill and woods again.*

# Southern Newspaper Accounts

Peter Wellington Alexander was a war correspondent for the *Savannah Republic* and the *Atlanta Southern Confederacy*. This article appears written verbatim with the exception of one historical mistake. The time of the Confederate artillery bombardment on Federal positions along Cemetery Ridge was at 1:00 o'clock in the afternoon not 10 o'clock in the morning. The following article was written on July 4, 1863.

*General Lee did not renew the attack the next day, the 3rd until ten o'clock when he opened upon the enemy from all parts of his line with over a hundred and forty guns. The enemy responded promptly and vigorously, using a great deal of round shot, his supply of shell, it may be, having been exhausted. So heavy an artillery fire was probably never heard before. Our guns were well served, as was shown by the ground around the Federal batteries, which was covered with dead men and horses. At quarter to three o'clock, and after the artillery had prepared the way, Pickett's Virginia division, Longstreet's corps, which had only arrived the night before, was ordered to assault Cemetery Hill, which was considered the key to the enemy's position. He was supported by Heth's division, commanded by Johnston Pettigrew and Wilcox's brigade, of Anderson's division, both belonging to Hill's corps. Pickett's charge was made in excellent order and gallant style, and he succeeded in wrestling a portion of the hill and the guns in that quarter from the enemy, but the enfilading fires which were brought to bear upon him, and the failure of Pettigrew to get up simultaneously with himself, rendered it necessary for him to retire with great loss. Of his brigadiers Gen. Garnett was killed, and left* on the field, Gen. Kemper mortally wounded, and since dead, and Gen. Armistead wounded. All of his field officers were struck, except two or three, and many of them killed.

The article below appeared in *The Richmond Daily Dispatch*. It was published on July 13, 1863. The article was written on the 1st Virginia Infantry's activity on the third day at Gettysburg. The 1st Virginia Infantry was from General Kemper's brigade of General Pickett's division.

*About 3 o'clock Friday morning the 1st Va. was ordered to fall in, and with the division march to the right of our center, nearly opposite the flanking mountain, and was placed behind our artillery. The cannon opened from our side about 1 o'clock, and after two hour's shelling, which was so inaccurate on the part of the enemy that only five men of the 1st were killed by it, the infantry was ordered to advance. The order was given at 3 o'clock P. M., and the advance was commenced, the infantry marching at common time across the field, and not firing a musket until within yards of the enemy's works. As Kemper's brigade moved up it swung around to the left and was exposed to the front fire and flanking fire of the Federals, which was very fatal. The swinging around unmasked a part of the enemy's force, five regiments being pushed out from the left to the attack. Directly this force was unmasked, our artillery opened on it with terrible precision. An officer who was within a few yards of the works informs that our change in position, by marching by the right, was thrown with wonderful accuracy into the very middle of the enemy's column killing sometimes as many as 20 or 30 at a shot. The force was advancing in column of battalion, and in tempting to change their position, by marching by the right, was thrown into such confusion by the scathing fire of our artillery that the slaughter was still more terrible. They never rallied, and their five regimental flags were scattered all about in the crowd. The demonstration on the offensive being dispersed our infantry continued their advance upon the works, when within about 75 yards they opened and charged on the fence. As they mounted the fence two or three hundred of the Yankees defending it threw down their arms and ran towards our men, giving themselves up as prisoners. Many of them ran entirely through Kemper's brigade to the rear. A good many of them were killed in running forward to surrender, our men not understanding the meaning.* The Confederates captured the works but so few of them passed through the deadly fire that not enough got inside to hold them against the large force of Yankees that advanced to retake them.

Seven Confederate flags were planted on the stone fence, but there not being enough men to support them were captured by the advancing Yankee force, and nearly all our severely wounded were left in the hands of the enemy.

## Gettysburg References

### Prologue

1) Never Call Retreat. Bruce Catton. Doubleday Publishing. Page 102-106.
2) The Road to Disunion. Volume II. William W. Freehling. Oxford University. Press. Page 524.
3) Valley News Echo. Volume II No. I April 1861. Front page and page 2.
4) Battles and Leaders Volume III. Century Magazine. Castle Publishing. Page 550.
5) Battles and Leaders Volume III. Century Magazine. General Joseph Johnston. Page 473, 481, 482.
6) Time Chart History of the Civil War. Lowe & B. Hould Publishers. Pages 45- 46, 47,49.
7) OR Series I, Volume LII/2. Governor John Pettus to President Jefferson Davis. Page 468.
8) Jefferson Davis The Man and His Hour. LSU Press. William C. Davis. Page 502, 504.
9) Rise and Fall. Volume II. Jefferson Davis. Pages 404-405.
10) OR Series I, Volume XXIV/1. General Joseph Johnston to Secretary of War James Seddon. Page 215.
11) Gettysburg. Stephen W. Sears. Houghton Mifflin. Page 10.
12) OR Series I. Volume XIXV/2. General Samuel Cooper to General Robert E. Lee. Page 720.
13) OR Series I, Volume XXV/2. General Lee to President Jefferson Davis. Page 791.
14) Gettysburg. Stephen W. Sears. Houghton Mifflin. Page 14.
15) Battles and Leaders Volume III. Century Magazine. Chancellorsville Campaign." Page 237, 437, 440.
16) Letter dated June 9, 1863. Major-General George Meade to his wife.
17) OR Series I, Volume XXVII/1. General-in-Chief Henry Halleck to General Meade. Page 61.
18) OR Series I, Volume XXVII/3. Secretary James Seddon to General Lee. Page 882.

19) Letter dated June 24, 1863. Major-General Dorsey Pender to his wife.
20) The Fremantle Diary. Buford. Lieutenant-Colonel James Fremantle. Page 199.
21) French Harding Civil War Memoirs. McClain. French Harding. Letter to Maggie Hutton. Page 248.
22) History of the 8th Virginia Infantry. H. E. Howard. Author James Devine. Page 19, Rooster.
23) Randolph Abbott Shotwell, Company F, 8th Virginia Infantry. Volume II. Hathi Library. Page 11.

## *Chapter One*

1) Jonathan Russell was a Confederate soldier. Regiment unknown. He is the grand uncle of the author. Courtesy of the Russell family.
2) Lee. Simon & Schuster. Douglas Southall Freeman. Page 185.
3) Amendment 13, Sections I and II, United States Constitution. Ratified December 6, 1865.
4) Six Years of Hell. LSU Press. Chester G. Hearn. Page 288.
5) John T. Trowbridge. The South: A Tour of Its Battle-Fields and Ruined Cities. Pages 62-68.
6) Reconstruction: America's Unfinished Revolution. Perennial. Eric Foner. Page xxiv.
7) OR Series I, Volume II. General Harper to General William Richardson. Page 773.
8) Battles and Leaders. Volume I. "Jackson at Harpers Ferry 1861." John D. Imboden. Page 120.
9) Valley News Echo. Volume II No. I April 1861. Front page, page 2.
10) This Hallowed Ground. Castle Books. Bruce Catton. Page 19-20, 252-253, 399.
11) A Confederate Surgeon's Letters to His Wife. Spencer Welch. Pages 55-57.
12) Letters of Private James Russell, Company A, 8th Virginia Infantry. June 22, 1863.
13) Pickett's Charge: The Last Attack at Gettysburg. UNC Press Earl J. Hess. Pages 6, 13.

## Chapter Two

1) Loudoun Discovered. Volume V. Thomas Balch Library. Eugene Scheel. Introduction.
2) The Russell family Tree. Courtesy Virginia Whitehair.
3) Loudoun Discovered. Volume V. Thomas Balch Library. Eugene Scheel. Pages 189-190.
4) The Strange Story of Harper's Ferry. Jefferson Publishing. Joseph Berry. Page 92.
5) History of Ebenezer United Methodist Church Pamphlet. Virginia Whitehair
6) "The raid of John Brown at Harper's Ferry as I saw it." Internet Archives. Pastor Samuel Leech. Page 2.
7) Russell family memoirs. Courtesy of Daisy Russell Wiles and Virginia Whitehair.
8) Farm Life in the 18th Century. History of Loudoun County. Eugene Scheel.

## Chapter Three

1) The Harpers Ferry Archives. Harpers Ferry and the Industrial Revolution. Pages 1, 3, 5.
2) John Brown's Trail. Harvard University Press. Brian McGinty. Pages 22, 56.
3) The Harpers Ferry Archives. The Historical Significance of Harpers Ferry. Pages 1,3, 4-5.
4) Six Years of Hell. LSU Press. Chester G. Hearn. Page 46.
5) The Strange Story of Harpers Ferry. Jefferson Publishing. Joseph Berry. Pages 35, 61, 84-86, 95.
6) "The raid of John Brown at Harper's Ferry as I saw it." Internet Archives. Samuel Leech. Pages 3, 5, 11, 14.
7) The Valley News Echo. Volume I, No. I. October 25, 1859. Front page.
8) Official Report by Colonel Robert E. Lee, United States Army. October 18, 1859.

## Chapter Four

1) The Strange Story of Harpers Ferry. Jefferson Publishing. Joseph Berry. Pages 66-68, 78.

2) The Valley News Echo. Volume I, No. II. December 1859. Front page.
3) Loudoun Discovered. Volume V. Thomas Balch Library. Eugene Scheel. Page 205.
4) Six Years of Hell. LSU Press. Chester G. Hearn. Pages 45-46.
5) John Brown's Trail. Harvard University Press. Brian McGinty. Page 45.
6) The Valley News Echo. Volume I, No. I. Page 3.

## *Chapter Five*

1) Loudoun Discovered. Volume V. Thomas Balch Library. Eugene Scheel. Page 203.
2) Storm Over the Land. Konecky & Konecky. Carl Sandburg. Pages 8, 10, 11.
3) The Road to Disunion. Volume II. William W. Freehling. Oxford University Press. Pages 12, 325, 346, 438.
4) OR Series I, Volume I, No. 25. "Operations in Charleston Harbor." James Chestnut, Page 60.
5) Harper's Weekly. Volume V, No. 226. April 27, 1861. Page 2.
6) The Strange Story of Harpers Ferry. Jefferson Publishing. Joseph Berry. Pages 96-99.
7) Six Years of Hell. LSU Press. Chester G. Hearn. Pages 47, 48, 65, 78.
8) Dissonance. Harcourt. David Detzer. Pages 44, 55.
9) History of the Eight Virginia Infantry. Virginia Historical Series. John Devine. Prologue.
10) I Rode with Stonewall. Chapel Hill. Henry Kyd Douglas. Page 5.
11) OR Series I, Volume II, No. 1. "Destruction of U. S. Armory at Harpers Ferry." Lieutenant Roger Jones. Pages 3-5.
12) Harpers Ferry Archives. Civil War at Harpers Ferry. Pages 1-2.
13) West Virginia Archives and History. "Destruction of the Harpers Ferry Armory." David Strothers.
14) Battles and Leaders. Volume I. Brigadier- General John

Imboden. Pages 120-121,124.
15) OR Series I, Volume II. Correspondence. Adjutant General S. Cooper to General Joseph Johnston. Pages 844-845, 924.
16) Stonewall Jackson. Barnes and Noble Books. G. F. R. Henderson. Page 87.
17) Bull Run to Bull Run. B. F. Jones Publishing. Captain George Baylor, 12th Virginia Cavalry. Pages 18-19.
18) Harpers Ferry Archives. Election Day 1860. Page 2.
19) The Stonewall Brigade. LSU Press. James Robertson. Pages 9, 248-249.
20) Battle at Bull Run. LSU Press. William C. Davis. Page 45.
21) OR Series I, Volume XIX/1, No. 202. "The Maryland Campaign." Page 49.
22) The Valley News Echo. Volume II. No. II. Page 4.
23) History of the Second Virginia Infantry. H. E. Howard Publishing. Dennis Frye. Pages 4-8.

## *Chapter Six*

1) I Rode with Stonewall. Chapel Hill Press. Henry Kyd Douglas. Chapter I Page 5.
2) Russell Family Memoirs. Virginia Wiles Whitehair.
3) Nothing but Victory. Vintage. Steven Woodworth. Chapter 1. Page 14.
4) The Civil War Times. Volume XLII, No. 5. Pages 38-39, 46.
5) The Strange Story of Harpers Ferry. Jefferson Publishing. Joseph Berry. Pages 119-120.
6) The Valley News Echo. Volume III, No. II. February 1862. Front page and page 3.
7) John T. Trowbridge. The South: A Tour of Its Battle-Fields and Ruined Cities. Pages 62-68.
8) Corporal Charles Moulton, 34th Massachusetts Infantry. Letter from Harpers Ferry to his mother, dated, July 19, 1863.
9) History of the Second Virginia Infantry. H. E. Howard Publishing. Dennis Frye. Page14, Rooster.

10) Four Years in the Stonewall Brigade. South Carolina Press. John O. Casler, Company A, 33rd Virginia Infantry. Pages 22.
11) OR Series I, Volume II, No.81. "Bull Run Campaign." General Joseph Johnston. Page 475.
12) OR Series I, Volume II, No.82. "Bull Run Campaign." Brigadier-General Thomas Jackson. Pages 481-482.
13) Battles and Leaders Volume III. Century Magazine. Composition and Losses of the Confederate Army. Page 195.
14) OR Series I, Volume II, No.84. "Bull Run Campaign." General P. G. T. Beauregard. Page 496.
15) The Lincoln Reader. Rutgers Press. Paul Angle. Chapter 5. Pages 377, 402.
16) Storm Over the Land. Konecky & Konecky. Carl Sandburg. Chapter 4. Page 168.

## *Chapter Seven*

1) History of the 2nd Virginia Infantry. Virginia Regimental Historical Series. H. E. Howard. Dennis E. Frye. Rooster.
2) Four Years in the Stonewall Brigade. South Carolina Press. John O. Casler. Pages 151,153.
3) The Lincoln Reader. Rutgers Press. Paul Angle. Chapter 5. Pages 377, 402.
4) Storm Over the Land. Konecky & Konecky. Carl Sandburg. Chapter 4. Page 168.
5) OR Series I, Volume XXV/1 No. 309. "Chancellorsville Campaign." General Robert E. Lee. Pages 798-799.
6) OR Series I, Volume XXV/1, No. 338. "Chancellorsville Campaign." Major-General Jeb Stuart. Page 887.
7) They Called Him Stonewall. Buford Books. Burke Davis. Chapter 24. Pages 448-449.
8) Lee's Lieutenants. One-Volume Abridgement, Stephen Sears. Chapter 24. Pages 526, 530, 534-535.

## *Chapter Eight*

1) The Stonewall Brigade. LSU Press. James Robertson.

Pages 186-187, 189, 196-198.
2) OR Series I, Volume XXV/1, No. 338. "Chancellorsville Campaign." Major- General Jeb Stuart. Page 889.
3) OR Series I, Volume XXV/1, No. 338. "Chancellorsville Campaign." Colonel J. S. Funk. Pages 1013-1014.
4) Four Years in The Stonewall Brigade. South Carolina Press. John Casler. Pages 164-165.
5) Papers of Randolph A. Shotwell, 8th Virginia Infantry. Three Years in Battle, Three Years in Prison. Volume II.
6) OR Series I, Volume XXVII/2, No. 565. "Gettysburg Campaign." Major-General Jeb Stuart. Pages 680-684.
7) Private James Russell, Company A, 8th Virginia Infantry. Letter to Harriet Russell, June 22,1863.
8) History of the 8th Virginia Infantry. H. E. Howard. Author James Devine. Page 19.

## *Chapter Nine*

1) Roads to Gettysburg. McClain Press. John Schildt. Pages 22, 40-41.
2) A Scythe of Fire. Perennial. Steven Woodworth. Pages 30-31.
3) Make Me A Map of The Valley. SMU Press. Diary of Jedediah Hotchkiss. Page 158.
4) Blue and Gray. Volume XXI, Issue 3. "Lee Steals A March on Joe Hooker, June 1863." Page 47.
5) The Stonewall Brigade. LSU Press. James Robertson. Page 198.
6) Four Years in The Stonewall Brigade. South Carolina Press. John Casler. Pages 165-167.
7) OR Series I, Volume XXVII/2, No. 488. Brigadier-General James Walker. Pages 516-518.
8) OR Series I, Volume XXVII/2, No. 489. Colonel J. Q. L. Nadenbousch. Pages 520-521.
9) Stonewall in The Valley. Stackpole Books. Robert Tanner. Pages 14-15.
10) Battles and Leaders. Volume III. Brevet Major-General

Henry Hunt. Pages 263-265.
11) History of the 56th Virginia Infantry. H. E. Howard. William and Patricia Young. Page 78.

## *Chapter Ten*

1) Virginia Country's Civil War. Volume I. Kate Sperry's Diary. Page 49.
2) A Women's Civil War. Wisconsin University Press. Diary of Cornelia McDonald. Pages 37, 155-158.
3) Winchester, Virginia: A Town Embattled During America's Civil War. Weider History Network.
4) Genteel Rebel: The Life of Mary Greenhow Lee. Southern Biography Series. Sheila Phipps.
5) Valley News Echo. Volume IV, No. VI. Front page and page 3.
6) Stonewall In The Valley. Stackpole Books. Robert Tanner. Pages 14-15.
7) The Stonewall Brigade. LSU Press. James Robertson. Page 249.
8) Roads to Gettysburg. McClain Press. John Schildt. Page 131.
9) The Fremantle Diary. Buford Books. Lieutenant-Colonel James Fremantle. Page 183.
10) History of the Second Virginia Infantry. H. E. Howard Publishing. Dennis Frye. Page 51.

## *Chapter Eleven*

1) A Scythe of Fire. Perennial. Steven Woodworth. Pages 213-214.
2) 9th Louisiana Infantry. Private William Rogers, Company I. Lieutenant James Small, Company I. 9th Louisiana Re-enactor's Website.
3) Southern Historical Society. Volume 24. Rev. J. William Jones. Page 147.
4) The Fremantle Diary. Buford. Lieutenant-Colonel James Fremantle. Page 179.
5) OR Series I, Volume XXVII/2. No. 383. "Gettysburg Campaign." Major- General R. H. Milroy. Pages 41-49.

6) OR Series I, Volume XXVII/2. No. 426. "The Gettysburg Campaign." General Robert E. Lee. Pages 313-315.
7) Lee's Tigers. LSU Press. Terry Jones. Pages 158-162.
8) History of the 8th Virginia Infantry. H. E. Howard. John Devine. Pages 1, 18- 19, 79.
9) History of the 1st Virginia Cavalry. H. E. Howard. Robert Driver. Page 23.
10) History of the 18th Virginia Infantry. H. E. Howard. James Robertson. Rooster.
11) Gettysburg. Houghton Mifflin. Stephen Sears. Pages 49, 52.
12) OR Series I, Volume XXVII/2. No. 472. Brigadier-General Harry Hays. Pages 476-477.

### *Chapter Twelve*

1) History of the 8th Virginia Infantry. H. E. Howard. John Devine. Prologue pages 3, 6, 9, 11, 16, 20.
2) A Scythe of Fire. Perennial. Steven Woodworth. Page 218.
3) Roads to Gettysburg. McClain Press. John Schildt. Page 164.
4) Gettysburg. Houghton Mifflin. Stephen Sears. Page 52.
5) The Fremantle Diary. Buford Books. Lieutenant-Colonel James Fremantle. Page 197.
6) General George Pickett. Civil War Biographies. Historical Times Encyclopedia of the Civil War.
7) General George Pickett Biography. The Pickett Society. Gettysburg, PA.
8) Lee's Cavalrymen. Stackpole Books. Edward Longacre. Page 201.
9) The Cavalry at Gettysburg. Bison Books. Edward Longacre. Pages 126-127, 129.
10) OR Series I, Volume XXVII/2. No. 565." Major-General Jeb Stuart. Pages 690-691.
11) General George Pickett in Life and Legend. UNC Press. Lesley Gordon. Pages 79-80, 106.
12) Pickett's Charge. Houghton Mifflin. George R. Stewart. Page 24.

13) History of the 18th Virginia Infantry. H. E. Howard. James Robertson. Page 20.

### *Chapter Thirteen*

1) A Scythe of Fire. Perennial. Steven Woodworth. Pages 220, 221-222, 223.
2) Battles and Leaders. Volume III. Castle. "Opposing Forces at Gettysburg. Page 437.
3) Pickett's Charge: The Last Attack at Gettysburg. Chapel Hill. Earl J. Hess. Pages 39, 41-42, 46.
4) The Freemantle Diary. Buford Books. Lieutenant-Colonel James Freemantle. Page 188.
5) Blue and Gray. Volume III, Issue VI. "The Battle Of Kernstown." Pages 28, 54.
6) I Rode with Stonewall. Chapel Hill. Henry Kyd Douglas. Page 245.
7) The Valley News Echo. Volume IV, No. VI. Page 4.
8) Papers of Randolph A. Shotwell. North Carolina Historical Commission. Pvt. Randolph Shotwell, 8th Virginia Infantry. Volume I, 483-484, 486.
9) Roads to Gettysburg. McClain Press. John Schildt. Pages 186-187.
10) OR Series I, Volume XXVII/2. No. 442. "The Gettysburg Campaign." Major James Dearing. Page 388.
11) History of the 8th Virginia Infantry. H. E. Howard. John Devine. Page 20.
12) History of the 56th Virginia Infantry. H. E. Howard. William and Patricia Young. Page 78.
13) History of the 18th Virginia Infantry. H. E. Howard. James Robertson. Page 20.

### *Chapter Fourteen*

1) History of the 8th Virginia Infantry. H. E. Howard. John Devine. Page 20.
2) Valley News Echo. Volume IV, No. VI Pages 1, 4.
3) General George Pickett in Life and Legend. UNC Press. Lesley Gordon. Page 109.
4) Nathaniel C. Wilson Diary. Virginia Military Institute.

June 26, 28, and July 1, 1863.
5) Roads to Gettysburg. McClain Press. John Schildt. Pages 220-221.
6) A Scythe of Fire. Perennial. Steven Woodworth. Page 224.
7) Four Years in The Stonewall Brigade. South Carolina Press. John Casler. Page 168.
8) Pickett's Charge: The Last Attack at Gettysburg. Chapel Hill. Earl J. Hess. Page 47.
9) Southern Historical Society. Volume XXXIV. Pickett's Charge. Page 328.
10) The Gettysburg Campaign. Simon & Schuster. Edwin Coddington. Page 171.
11) OR Series I, Volume XXVII/3. Confederate Correspondence. General Order # 72. Pages 912-913.
12) The Philadelphia Inquirer. Wednesday, July 1, 1863. Front page.
13) Peter Wellington Alexander. Chambersburg, PA. June 26, 1863.
14) OR Series I, Volume XXVII/2. No. 426. General Robert E. Lee. Page 426.
15) History of the 56th Virginia Infantry. H. E. Howard. William and Patricia Young. Pages 78-79.

## *Chapter Fifteen*

1) History of the 8th Virginia Infantry. H. E. Howard. John Devine. Pages 21, 24.
2) Pickett's Charge. Houghton Mifflin. George Stewart. Pages 4, 5, 25, 29- 30.
3) America's Civil War. July 2006. Page 32.
4) Witness to Gettysburg. Meridian. Richard Wheeler.
5) OR Series I, Volume XXVII/2. No. 426. General Robert E. Lee. Pages 298-299, 308.
6) OR Series I, Volume XXVII/2. No. 430. General James Longstreet. Pages 358-359.
7) Gettysburg Day Three. Touchstone. Jeffery Wert. Page 32.
8 Papers of Randolph A. Shotwell. North Carolina Historical Commission. Pvt. Randolph Shotwell, 8th

Virginia Infantry. Chapter 32. Page 2.
9) Letter. Assistant Surgeon William Taylor, 19th Virginia.

## *Chapter Sixteen*

1) Pickett's Charge: The Last Attack at Gettysburg. Chapel Hill. Earl J. Hess. Pages 48, 153, 155-156.
2) Papers of Randolph A. Shotwell. North Carolina Historical Commission. Pvt. Randolph Shotwell, 8th Virginia Infantry. Chapter 32. Pages 4-5, 8.
3) Gettysburg Day Three. Touchstone. Jeffery Wert. Pages 95, 113-114.
4) The Freemantle Diary. Buford. Lieutenant-Colonel James Freemantle. Page 198.
5) Battles and Leaders. Volume III. Lieutenant-Colonel E P. Alexander. Page 363.
6) History of the 8th Virginia Infantry. H. E. Howard. John Devine. Pages 1, 21-22.
7) Brigades of Gettysburg. Da Capo Press. Bradley Gottfried. Page 479.
8) Pickett's Charge. Houghton Mifflin. George Stewart. Page 135.
9) Witness to Gettysburg. Meridian. Richard Wheeler. Pages 233, 235.
10) Peter Wellington Alexander. July 4, 1863.
11) OR Series I, Volume XXVII/2. No. 426. General Robert E. Lee. Page 308.
12) OR Series I, Volume XXVII/2. No. 430. General James Longstreet. Page 359.
13) OR Series I, Volume XXVII/2. No. 442. Major James Dearing. Page 388-389.
14) OR Series I, Volume XXVII/2. No. 441. Major Charles Peyton. Page 389.
15) OR Series I, Volume XXVII/2. No. 464. Lieutenant-Colonel E. P. Alexander. Pages 430-431.
16) OR Series I, Volume XXVII/2. No. 466. Major B. F. Eshelman. Pages 434-435.
17) OR Series I, Volume XXVII/2. No. 534. General A. P. Hill. Page 608.

18) OR Series I, Volume XXVII/2. No. 535. Colonel Lindsey Walker. Page 610.
19) Southern Historical Society Papers. Volume IV. Colonel E. P. Alexander.
20) Southern Historical Society Papers. Volume XXXII. The "Old First" Virginia at Gettysburg.
21) Southern Historical Society Papers. Volume XXXII. Colonel Rawley Martin.
22) Southern Historical Society Papers. Volume XXXII. Gettysburg Pickett's Charge. 1905, 1906.
24) Richmond Times Dispatch. May 6, 1906. Colonel Joseph C. Mayo, 3rd Virginia Infantry.
25) History of the 56th Virginia Infantry. H. E. Howard. William and Patricia Young. Page 79.
26) Blue and Gray. Volume V, Issue VI. Page 35.
27) The Stonewall Brigade. Articles on food preparations.

## *Chapter Seventeen*

1) History of the 56th Virginia Infantry. H. E. Howard. William and Patricia Young. Page 81-82.
2) Gettysburg Day Three. Touchstone. Jeffery Wert. Page 95.
3) Pickett's Charge: The Last Attack at Gettysburg. Chapel Hill. Earl J. Hess. Pages 168-169.
4) Pickett's Charge. Houghton Mifflin. George Stewart. Pages 168-169.
5) History of the 18th Virginia Infantry. H. E. Howard. James Robertson. Page 21.
6) Papers of Randolph A. Shotwell. North Carolina Historical Commission. Pvt. Randolph Shotwell, 8th Virginia Infantry. Chapter 32. Pages 9-12.
7) The Battle of Gettysburg Special Issue. Sovereign Media Company. Page 67.
8) Gettysburg. Houghton Mifflin. Stephen Sears. Pages 415, 421.
9) Nathaniel C. Wilson Diary. Virginia Military Institute. July 3, 1863.
10) Southern Historical Society Papers. Volume XXXIII. "Gettysburg Pickett's Charge."

11) Battles and Leaders. Volume III. "Lee's Right Wing at Gettysburg." General James Longstreet. Page 346.
12) Personal Recollections of General Edward Porter Alexander. Chapel Hill. Page 263.
13) General Longstreet The Confederacy's Most Controversial Soldier. Touchstone. Jeffry Wert. Page 289.
14) The Gettysburg Campaign. Touchstone. Edward B. Coddington. Page 502.
15) OR Series I, Volume XXVII/2. No. 28. General Henry Hunt. Page 239.
16) Peter Wellington Alexander. Gettysburg. July 4, 1863.
17) Brigades of Gettysburg. Da Capo Press. Bradley Gottfried. Page 480.
18) Richmond Times Dispatch. September 28, 1936. Captain Frank Nelson, Company A, 56th Virginia Infantry.
19) Contributions to a History of the Richmond Howitzer Battalion. Page 208.

## *Chapter Eighteen*

1) History of the 56th Virginia Infantry. H. E. Howard. William and Patricia Young. Pages 84-85.
2) Papers of Randolph A. Shotwell. North Carolina Historical Commission. Pvt. Randolph Shotwell, 8th Virginia Infantry. Pages 12-13, 19.
3) Gettysburg Day Three. Touchstone. Jeffery Wert. Pages 95, 197-198, 205, 212-213.
4) Southern Historical Society Papers. Volume XXXI. Captain Robert Bright.
5) History of the 8th Virginia Infantry. H. E. Howard. John Devine. Pages 22-24.
6) Pickett's Charge. Houghton Mifflin. George Stewart. Pages 184, 187, 198, 205.
7) Pickett's Charge: The Last Attack at Gettysburg. Chapel Hill. Earl J. Hess. Page 171.
8) The Gettysburg Campaign. Simon & Schuster. Edwin Coddington. Page 502.
9) History of the 18th Virginia Infantry. H. E. Howard.

James Robertson. Pages 21-23.
10) Blue and Gray. Volume XXVI, Issue IV. Pages 41, 43.
11) History of the 14th Connecticut Infantry. Charles Page. Page 151.
12) Peter Wellington Alexander. Gettysburg. July 4, 1863.
13) OR Series I, Volume XXVII/2. No. 426. General Robert E. Lee. Pages 310-311, 321.
14) OR Series I, Volume XXVII/2. Page 360.
15) OR Series I, Volume XXVII/2. Page 386.
16) OR Series I, Volume XXVII/2. Page 239.
17) OR Series I, Volume XXVII/2. Meade. Page 117.
18) OR Series I, Volume XXVII/2. Stannard Page 359-360.
19) OR Series I, Volume XXVII/2. Scott Hancock. Pages 373-374.
20) OR Series I, Volume XXVII/2. Hays. Page 454.
21) OR Series I, Volume XXVII/2. McGilvery. Pages 883-884.
22) OR Series I, Volume XXVII/2.
23) Southern Historical Society Papers. Vol. XLI. R. Talcott. Sept. 1916.
24) Lee. Touchstone. Douglas Southall Freeman. Page 339.

## *Chapter Nineteen*

1) Pickett's Charge. Houghton Mifflin. George Stewart. Pages 216-217, 219.
2) History of the 8th Virginia Infantry. H. E. Howard. John Devine. Page 24.
3) Pickett's Men. Walter Harrison, A. A. and Inspector for General George Pickett's Division. Pages 98-99.
4) History of the 56th Virginia Infantry. H. E. Howard. William and Patricia Young. Page 86.
5) History of the 18th Virginia Infantry. H. E. Howard. James Robertson. Pages 21, 23.
6) Pickett's Charge: The Last Attack at Gettysburg. Chapel Hill. Earl J. Hess. Page 251.
7) Blue and Gray. Volume XXVI, Issue IV. Pages 43, 49.
8) Papers of Randolph A. Shotwell. North Carolina Historical Commission. Pvt. Randolph Shotwell, 8th

Virginia Infantry. Pages 13, 15, 19, 24.
9) Gettysburg Day Three. Touchstone. Jeffery Wert. Page 290.
10) Witness to Gettysburg. Meridian. Richard Wheeler. Pages 243, 256.
11) Peter Wellington Alexander. Gettysburg, July 4, 1863.
12) Peter Wellington Alexander. Gettysburg. July 7, 1863.
13) Valley News Echo, Volume IV, No. VII. Page 2.
14) Battles and Leaders. Volume III. Castle. "The Charge of Pickett, Pettigrew, and Tremble." J. B. Smith. Pages 390-391.
15) Battles and Leaders. Volume III. Castle. "Lee's Right Wing at Gettysburg. General James Longstreet. Page 347.
16) OR Series I, Volume XXVII/2. No. 76. Major-General Winfield Scott Hancock. Page 374.
17) OR Series I, Volume XXVII/2. No. 57. Colonel Theodore Gates, 80th New York Infantry. Pages 318-319.
18) OR Series I, Volume XXVII/2. No. 104. "The Gettysburg Campaign."
    Brigadier-General Alexander Webb. Page 428.
19) OR Series I, Volume XXVII/2. No. 105. Captain William Davis, 69th Pennsylvania Infantry. Page 431.
20) OR Series I, Volume XXVII/2. No. 441. Major Charles Peyton. Page 387.
21) OR Series I, Volume XXVII/2. No. 608. General A. P. Hill. Page 609.

## *Chapter Twenty*

1) Lee. Touchstone. Douglas Southhall Freeman. Page 341.
2) The Freemantle Diary. Buford. Lieutenant-Colonel James Freemantle. Pages 212-213.
3) Pickett's Charge. Houghton Mifflin. George Stewart. Pages 256-257, 263.
4) Gettysburg Day Three. Touchstone. Jeffery Wert. Page 291.
5) Papers of Randolph A. Shotwell. North Carolina

Historical Commission. Pvt. Randolph Shotwell, 8th
Virginia Infantry. Pages 25, 27.
6) Battles and Leaders. Volume III. Castle. "Opposing Forces at Gettysburg." Page 437.
7) History of the 8th Virginia Infantry. H. E. Howard. John Devine. Page 25.
8) Make Me A Map of The Valley. SMU Press. Jed Hotchkiss. July 3, 1863. Pages 157-158.
9) Southern Historical Society Papers. Volume XXXI. Captain Robert Bright.

## Newspapers

1) Philadelphia Inquirer. July 7, 1863.
2) Harper's Weekly. July 25, 1863.
3) Atlanta Southern Confederacy and The Savannah Republic. Peter Wellington. July 4, 1863.
4) The Richmond Daily Dispatch. July 13, 1863.

Made in the USA
Columbia, SC
08 October 2021